The Amazing Adventures
of
Dexter and Dood

The Puzzle

S.L. Hill

This edition published in Great Britain in 2014 by
Farthings Publishing,
8 Christine House
1 Avenue Victoria
SCARBOROUGH
YO11 2QB
UK

http://www.Farthings-Publishing.com

info@farthings.org.uk

ISBN 978-1-291-62157-0

March 2014 (h)

FOR MY MUM WHO LOVED TO READ

AND FOR MY THREE SPECIAL PEOPLE WHO LIT THE
FLAME

SOPHIE

JOSEPH

OLIVIA

AND TO DEXTER – FOR JUST BEING YOU!

CHAPTER 1

Through the undergrowth, in the dusky night sky, skulked a fierce nasty beast preparing to pounce on his unsuspecting prey. He believed he owned this territory. All creatures bowed down to his greatness – they cowered in his presence and acted upon his every purr.

Once he had terrorised all creatures great and small, he slithered back to his indulgent castle, scratched his talons upon the plush rug and curled up for his slumber to begin. His castle was like no other...risen high above the Earth suspended in thin air on a cloud. No expense had been spared on the quality of the furnishings, wooden and strong; extensive gardens provided exercise and shelter and the quality of the food was simply exquisite. From this position on the cloud he looked down on all the earthlings fighting for space on the tiny planet below. He basked in the heat of a spherical fire ball and watched the wonders of shooting stars and asteroids for entertainment. High above the sky he felt like the Ruler of the Universe.

And then he woke up!

Kasper K. Itty was a cat and a fat one at that! A round, ginger fur ball that lived with his master, Old Rufus Rule, in a dusty cottage on the edge of a spooky wood. Daily, lazy Kasper mooched around the house, ignoring the mischievous mice and eating stale misshapen biscuits. Old Rufus rocked in his chair by the open fire watching a square box on the wall. Kasper was Rufus' only friend and he loved him dearly; unfortunately this love was not reciprocated. He allowed Kasper to wander each room of the house, looking for somewhere soft to sleep, which he did for at least ten hours each day.

"An old, run down house ... infested with ... at least one mouse."

CHAPTER 2

That was anywhere.....apart from the room under the house – the cellar! The doorway into this room had a metal chain secured around it and five extensive locks: two at the top, two at the bottom and one in the middle to secure the chain. Old Rufus always wore the five keys on a rusty chain around his left ankle and wouldn't let anyone, but himself, into the room. Every evening without fail, he would spend one hour in this room. The noises that came from under this door would intrigue even the least nosy of humans.

When Kasper searched the house for somewhere comfortable and free of dust to sleep, he often sat in front of the locked door staring up at it, checking every centimetre of the flat white surface, trying to imagine a way in. He had to keep a careful look out for Old Rufus though, as he had been warned many times not to go anywhere near the door. But Kasper believed he was a brave, curious and naughty feline who liked dangerous adventures!

So one wintery evening, Kasper lay by the roaring open fire beside his owner's feet, pretending to be fast asleep. He had devised a cunning plan to get into the secret cellar. Rather than relying on his poor memory or paper to showcase his ingenious idea - he drew a clever map of his plan on his left paw.

Old Rufus rose from his chair at the usual time of twenty past seven, bent to his feet and untied the key chain; walking slowly to the locked door at the back of the house next to the rickety fridge.

As soon as Old Rufus was out of sight, Kasper opened one of his eyes to check that the old man had left the room. As spritely as a hefty cat could: he jumped from the floor to the chair, onwards to the ancient chandelier and then the wooden plinth above the door that led to the kitchen where Old Rufus was halfway through unlocking the five different locks. Kasper stood there still, flat against the wall so that he wouldn't be spotted. The plinth displayed Old Rufus' ghastly plate and teapot collection from the four corners of the world.

As the final lock snapped open, Old Rufus tugged at the stubborn door. It creaked open slowly allowing the light from the kitchen to penetrate the black abyss of the cellar, casting a long shadow of Rufus down the stone stairway. Three seconds to wait....2 seconds..... and just at the right moment as Rufus stepped into the blackness, Kasper nudged the favoured teapot from Sri Lanka with his wet sniffy nose. The teapot rocked backwards and forwards on the plinth until it could rock no more; tipping silently over the edge where gravity took control pulling the teapot to the solid oak floor below. Energetically Kasper pounced from the plinth to the kitchen worktop behind the toaster and crouched low, watching the teapot fall to its resting place with an almighty smash!

The sound echoed in Rufus' ears and he turned his head, stepping backwards out of the dark stairwell. He ran with thunderous strides to the shattered pieces of his teapot and fell to his knees – a sad sobbing noise emitting from his chest. Simultaneously, Kasper took the opportunity to jump silently to the floor and crept slowly into the darkness.

Old Rufus stared at the pieces of broken teapot, picking up the largest section, tears rolling down his weathered face, memories of his time in Sri Lanka flooding back.

CHAPTER 3

Kasper stood still at the top of the steep steps leading to the unknown below. He waited for his eyes to become accustomed to the blackness around him. Kasper felt frightened - his heart was beating loudly in his chest and his long, orange fur stood on end in fear. Swallowing hard, he knew he had to move fast before Old Rufus caught him and foiled his crafty plan.

Down he went, slowly and for once in his safe life he threw caution to the wind and pounced down the stairs like a tiger; even though he had no idea what would greet him at the bottom of the staircase, but he had spent the last two years waiting and guessing and this was his chance and he was determined to take it! No matter how frightened he was! Suddenly behind him, the door at the top of the steps slammed shut and extinguished the light! Kasper was plunged into pitch blackness and he sat and waited, unable to do anything else.

Finally he heard a rasp and crackle of a struck match and saw Old Rufus' face lit by the slender candle held in his hand, the heavy thud of his feet echoed as he descended the steps. Kasper jumped into the unknown darkness and watched Old Rufus come closer. As he reached the floor, the secret of the hidden room was released to Kasper as the candlelight bounced around the walls of the cellar. It was empty! There was nothing there! Kasper moved stealthily into one of the corners of the room, making himself disappear into the darkness.

Old Rufus knelt in the centre of the room and used his shovel-like hands to clear away some of the gravel and dirt covering the stone floor. As he continued to smooth and run his hands over the same small area on the floor, an extraordinary thing happened. Kasper had to blink twice and once more hard for three seconds, to ensure that he wasn't dreaming. As Old Rufus' hands moved back and forth; a small circular grey disk appeared in the floor from nowhere. Old Rufus knew this ritual well. He knocked on the disk twice with his deformed bulky knuckles and whispered...."Deo, deo, click, bow." The disk creaked as it clicked reluctantly twice to the left, once to the right and then rose up from the floor in front of Rufus, leaving a circular hole in the dusty floor. The hole was just large enough for one of Kasper's pesky mice to slip down.

Old Rufus sat cross legged by the hole obediently and closed his eyes. He slowly lifted his arms so that they were straight out in front of him and held them there in mid air. He clapped his hands above his head powerfully three loud times and lowered them in a controlled manner back to the floor, beside his legs. Eyes still firmly closed, he began to hum quietly under his breath whist raising his stretched arms palms towards the ceiling once more. The humming became louder over several minutes and finally a small blue and green object peeped through the hole in the floor. The object rose slowly, suspended in mid air, in front of Rufus' closed eyes. Kasper's eyes were as wide as saucers by now and he was finding it difficult to keep his curiosity under control.

He was about to consider moving out of the darkness when Rufus spoke. "Kasper come here..." he commanded in a firm, impatient voice.

Kasper gulped nervously. Now he knew he would be in deep trouble, he had been rumbled!

He may Look cute ... but he is an evil brute!

CHAPTER 4

"Sit down Kasper," he asked forcefully, as Kasper plodded reluctantly into the centre of the room, placing himself into an uncomfortable seated position, tail hugged closely to his body for comfort, facing his master.

"Do you know what this is Kasper?" he asked seemingly cross, pointing to the floating object.

"Mmmm, No Master, I do not," Kasper purred cunningly to Old Rufus.

"Please don't be frightened," he explained mellowing in his anger and appearing grateful to share something so important, "this object in front of you is the key to the whole universe: the final piece of a magical jigsaw puzzle. I should have shared this with you before now but I didn't know whether I could trust you. In the wrong hands, this jigsaw piece could change everything you see, feel and experience."

"I don't understand Sir, how can something so small affect everything we know?" Kasper quizzed tilting his body towards the suspended piece of coloured wood.

Old Rufus relaxed his seated position and explained, "When I was a young man, I had a dream, a very significant dream....That one day I would be given an object that I was to protect forever. I was the chosen one, the one trusted to keep the universe safe and balanced. And amazingly so, true to form, ten and a half years later, just before my Father died he dropped a mysterious object into my hand. I knew there and then that I had an important job to do. I have protected this jigsaw piece since it was delivered to me 46 years ago." Rufus looked somehow relieved after sharing such an overwhelming secret that he had kept for so long.

"But....how does this control the universe?" Kasper asked, extremely intrigued as to the apparent power of the object in front of him.

"It is possible in a way I cannot share, to travel to a dark sky above you," he explained, pointing upwards towards the ceiling, "there is a place, a control station in the deep, night sky which commands all the galaxies and planets in the universe. Planet Earth, this planet, is the busiest planet and has the most humans, creatures, plants living on it and therefore needs the most protection. Each planet was made many, many years ago by millions of these pieces," he pointed to the suspended jigsaw piece, "some planets were formed with yellow pieces, some red, some blue and green and so on. It is possible to change the pieces of the jigsaw within the control station and in turn determine exactly what happens on that planet potentially destroying everything and everyone. However, to make any changes the control station needs to be complete; what you see before you Kasper.... is that final controlling piece. Currently the control station cannot be altered as this final piece is missing – hence the importance of my role. I have independently kept the universe from any harm for all these years," he said boldly and proudly.

The cogs in Kasper's brain were turning very fast indeed right now. He had always thought that he was destined for a greater life of splendour and riches, rather than being a cute and cuddly pet belonging to a grumpy old man.

"Why would there be a spare piece? Why would the universe need to be saved or altered?" Kasper whispered one final question.

Rufus began to move his body into a standing position, bones and joints creaking as he explained quietly, "There are many evil people outside of these four walls Kasper that you won't understand. And this extra jigsaw piece may be needed one day only in the most desperate circumstances, when the whole universe could be threatened. It is my job and now yours too, to protect it with our lives until that day; if it ever happens."

Kasper sat and listened to every word: a plot – a clever nasty, evil plot was forming piece by piece in his developing cruel mind. "This little jigsaw piece could help me take over this boring, silly universe with rules that must be obeyed and followed. Kasper K. Itty's exciting universe where bossy humans and smelly mice don't exist could be just around the corner," he thought to himself with a wicked smile from ear to ear.

A mysterious piece ... colourful at least ...

CHAPTER 5

Dexter Dog sat on his favourite step. Seven steps from the bottom on the plush cream carpet, tummy on step seven, two front legs flopped onto step six and two back legs tucked under his body ready to pounce like springs. His head pointing towards the front of the house, looking through the open banister so that he could see everything that goes on outside and inside, especially checking out strangers walking past the house through the bay window - for suitability near his patch!

Dexter lived in a house in a country called England, somewhere by the sea. He had to share his house with lots of noisy people. A bossy but funny girl called Sophie – whose head was constantly in a book. Yuk! Another younger smiley girl called Olivia who was well... a bit of a Princess. (As the youngest she got away with almost anything with a wry smile and twinkle of her blue eyes) and a boy named Joseph; who wanted to be a superhero. Oh and of course Mum and Dad – the crumblies! This story is all about Joseph, a six year old small boy with bright ginger, spiky hair, freckles and the most vibrant imagination. Unfortunately for Joseph he had one of those cute faces that grown-ups, especially Granny, liked to pinch or kiss his cheeks. (This was not a good thing... Granny's face had huge red lips and a large wart on the end of her nose). Granny had also given Joseph the most frightful nickname as a cute cuddly baby that had remained with him for the next six years and he absolutely HATED it! "Doodle-doos." As soon as he heard the 'D' he curled up his nose, placed his fingers in his ears and refused to listen.

Fortunately over recent years, Doodle-Doos had been shortened to Dood, which he could tolerate, just! However, the other unfortunate occurrence was that Joseph was well... SHORT! (compared to his peers) and because of this, combined with his nickname, Joseph was known by all as Dinky Dood!

Dexter and Dood were the very best of buddies. They ate together, slept together, played together and most importantly spoke to each other, sharing TOP secrets.

Dood knew everything about Dexter and Dexter knew everything about Dood. They had to keep their communication a secret from the smelly girls and crumblies in the house; as Dexter only barked and looked daft to them, fetching sticks and rolling onto his back for a tummy tickle. Dood found his 'acting' hilarious and they often joked about it when everyone else was sound asleep.

We should probably explain how Dexter dog came to live with this particular family some three years ago. One evening Mum had questioned Dad about how she looked in her new rosy red dress. Rather foolishly Dad's response had not been as practised as usual (he was distracted by Top Gear) and he sounded a little negative! And from that moment on, Mum had decided drastic action was required to ensure she became as fit and healthy as she was twenty years ago, hence the purchasing of Dexter.

Unfortunately for Dexter, as much as he liked his morning walks; the sight of Mum in sporting attire was enough to put anyone off their meaty chunks! Sweat band, wrist bands, leg warmers, extremely short shorts, trainers, Ipod and large, black sunglasses. Everything but the sunglasses was.....you guessed it...PINK! Vivid, garish pink! So pink, anyone coming the other way would be sure to get an instant headache!

Dexter tried everything he knew to avoid this morning torture! Faking illness (including death), injury, hiding and running away. All failed, Mum found him every time and in whatever condition he was in, attached the pink collar and lead and out they went onto the road for all to see.

Dexter tolerated this ridicule for three weeks and one day, until he could take it no more, as he had become the laughing stock of the puppy community. As Mum ran (it looked more like a dizzy spider jumping on hot coals) that morning, they came up to the lake at the side of the wood when Dexter decided he needed to stop this torture once and for all. As Mum and Dexter picked up speed, near the deepest part of the lake, Dexter suddenly stopped to smell the juicy grass at his feet. Sadly for Mum, she did not see this coming and as the lead tightened she flew high into the air, somersaulted beautifully and landed face first in the lake, bottom in the air, disturbing the sleeping ducks.

Dexter looked up, practising his 'shocked' expression at what had happened and sat obediently by the side of the lake, whilst Mum pulled herself to shore. The tickly laugh in his tummy was difficult to control and he was getting a belly ache, as he tried to suppress the giggles at what he saw in front of him. Unbelievably, Mum didn't look quite as pink and perfect anymore! (apart from her cheeks with embarrassment). She stomped, dripping wet, towards Dexter not saying a single word, picked up his lead and headed for home. Dexter looked suitably sorrowful until he heard the words that were magic to his ears! "I am never taking you running with me ever again, you bad dog!" Now that made Dexter smile! From that point forward Dood and Dexter have taken each other for 'walks' of adventure.

Dood (and Dexter's) bedroom was strictly a 'boys only' zone at the very top of the house in the loft. Rudely, Dood had labelled his door with:

IF YOU LIKE PINK
YOU aRe a BIT OF a STINK
KeeP ouT OR eLSe
You HaVe BeeN WaRNeD

Just for extra security Dood and Dexter had rigged together an alarm system. If the door handle happened to be touched, it would buzz and vibrate loudly as well as shout a recording from Dood blasting 'BOYS ONLY: BAD LUCK! GO AWAY!' Finally, the most gigantic water bomb suspended high above the door frame filled with one quarter water, a quarter pond slim, one quarter liquid soap (Mum's best of course) and a final quarter of

Granny's thick disgusting lumpy custard, tied to a very thin string from the ceiling. Just by the light switch inside Dood's room, was the master water bomb drop switch. Dood couldn't wait for his first victim, but unfortunately no one was ever stood there long enough to get dumped on or not yet anyway!

The crumblies and girlies had given up trying to get in! Instead they passed pink notes under the door if they wanted anything. Dood and Dex read them with binoculars being sure not to contaminate themselves with pinkness, and then threw them out of the window once read!

The duo liked adventures. Rather unfortunately they didn't always turn out quite as planned. Instead they often got themselves into a spot of bother with Dad or the neighbour with his pointy nose and flashy red car or received a few cuts and bruises escaping from dangerous situations. However this never put them off! Dex and Dood both shared an amazing dream that one day they would both be superheroes. Real, flying, power packed magical heroes, wearing cool body armour suits, hiding their identity with masks, utilising magical powers to combat evil and use a range of gadgets to catch those doing wrong.

Dex slept at the foot of Dood's wooden cabin bed, keeping Dood's toes toasty warm in the cold, wintery night. Dexter lay in his favoured position on his back stretched out like a banana with all four paws high in the air, nose pointing towards the ceiling and ears flat against the duvet, eyes almost closed. Dood's bed was like any other ordinary cabin bed with a mattress, duvet and pillows on the highest section but hidden underneath was their adventure planning station. A blue curtain kept the station extra secure from nosy outsiders. Inside the adventure station were wall to wall plans of ideas, pictures, maps and designs. On the planning table was a collection of model gadgets that Dex and Dood spent their time creating and making. This area was where Dex and Dood spent all of their time perfecting how to be superheroes: how they would save the world if needed, what gadgets they would need and what they would wear to disguise themselves. (This was extremely important to get the esteemed title of superhero...You've seen batman, superman....similar idea!) As they slept soundly that night, they dreamt the same exciting adventure. Dood was dressed in his shiny blue lycra superhero costume, including mask, silky cape, gadget belt and pockets. He sat on Dexter's back flying through the tall maze of buildings, chasing an evil furry cat that flew at speed on a cloud, firing balls of fire, dust and water. Dexter also dressed in mask, cloak and gadget collar swiftly dodged the balls as Dood fired water from his gadget gun.

Every morning over breakfast, Dex and Dood shared their dreams - unfortunately they were always the same: chasing the bad guys....but never actually capturing their prey!

CHAPTER 6

Some distance away, Kasper had spent the past three cold wintery months devising how he could steal the magical jigsaw piece. He didn't know very much about its power but knew it would be used towards a much better cause (his own!!) if it was in his furry paws rather than Old Rufus' possession. Kasper firmly believed it was such a waste of something so powerful, locked away in a stuffy cellar of an old house. He just couldn't understand why Old Rufus hadn't used the jigsaw piece to make himself strong and powerful and ultimately the Ruler of the Planet. And if Rufus didn't want to take up such a phenomenal opportunity..... then he would instead! He saw himself as a bit of an opportunist and this was just the opportunity he had spent his whole life waiting for.

After the broken teapot episode, Kasper had realised very quickly that he would not be allowed within ten metres of the cellar ever again. (The chains had been replaced by an expensive finger print and eye scanning system the very next day.) Old Rufus never mentioned the jigsaw again to Kasper. He was also extra careful when anywhere near the cellar door to ensure that no one was following him into that sacred room. Kasper had been ignored by his owner for quite some time since the incident. Consequently he had spent most of his time outside in the overgrown garden area of the house, away from Old Rufus.

Kasper's 'brilliant' idea came to him as he perched in the old apple tree, one very ordinary sunny morning. What do cats do well? They chase, dig and bury. A digging and burying plan was the order of the day — true brilliance! Logically, Kasper worked out roughly from the tree where he was sat, where the cellar was positioned deep under the garden, he counted in mouse lengths, a measurement he knew like the back of his paw. He lazily jumped down from the tree and surveyed the ground. Kasper was content that he would be quite safe outside, as Old Rufus only came out of the house once a week on a Thursday to walk to the local shops and he was gone for one hour only, not a minute more. After careful calculations, Kasper placed an X on the floor and began to dig with his front furry paws and after five minutes of digging he realised that this plan was not going to happen over night! It was going to take a while to execute and was also going to be quite tiring for a kitty of his years.

Kasper was a clever but very lazy cat — possibly the laziest cat you have ever come across. If he could sit around and do nothing, he would! He was also very resourceful. He needed to dig a deep tunnel under the ground, leading to the cellar and knock out enough of the bricks to allow him to collect the puzzle piece. Advantageously, he happened to know most of the local kittens, mice and a few small dumb dogs that lived nearby. He sent out a note with one of the dutiful mice and found, mostly out of fear, that he had an 'enthusiastic' working party most days to dig his hole for him. Kasper welcomed the role of supervisor from the apple tree, shouting commands to those minions below him.

Within three frustrating months the tunnel was complete.

Two of the mice scurried down the passageway with hammers and chisels to carefully and quietly dislodge the bricks ready for the Thursday hour Rufus free time tomorrow morning. The day of freedom had arrived at last!! Kasper knew he would be leaving tomorrow to start a new life and what a life it would be!

He was convinced that the magical jigsaw piece would make all his dreams come true and he could not wait to get started. "If only Rufus had told me how the magical jigsaw piece actually worked, what powers it has and how all of this is possible... the opportunities are well, just endless," he thought to himself arrogantly (not at all despondent with the lack of key information), eyes bright and wide as he lazed on the widest tree branch, waiting for night to fall, knowing that tomorrow would be the beginning of the rest of his life.

CHAPTER 7

The next brilliant sunny morning, Kasper silently hid behind the old oak tree. He was so, so ready for this moment. "Come on Rufus, get up and out to the shops and let me get on with finding this piece of pure magic!" he purred to himself cunningly, tail wagging with impatience.

Sure enough, as predicted a moment later, Old Rufus opened the ramshackled front door with a creak and slammed it shut behind him and off he stomped wearily, shopping bags in his hands. From behind his hiding place, Kasper skulked forwards. He commanded the mice to come with him to the hole that was hidden with a plant pot, containing smelly pink roses. Exhausted, the mice struggled to pull the plant pot away from the hole whilst Kasper watched, rubbing his paws together eagerly.

Once the pot had been moved, Kasper placed all four paws on the grass and looked down the black tunnel engineered by the mice workers. He was a clever, curious devious cat but he wasn't exactly the bravest feline in the world. As he looked down the black tunnel into the darkness below, he gulped hard as he realised he was frightened but he knew he had to find the magical jigsaw piece.

Fortunately for Kasper he liked eating. Unfortunately he didn't like exercise. And so over the years, he had increased his size quite phenomenally; consequently his bottom was the widest part of his body. The hole had been made by tiny mice and spritely kittens and so as Kasper embarked on his journey cautiously down the tunnel it became narrower towards the end. Slowly, as he squeezed towards his prize; Kasper's wide furry rear became firmly stuck, lodged in the tunnel. He couldn't go backwards or forwards and the bricks, the entrance to his newly found freedom, was a stretched paw away. Kasper tried with all his might to move his immense body further forwards but he was well and truly stuck!

The frightened animals above ground saw what was happening and began chuckling. The laugh began with a tiny chuckle in the throat and developed into a rip roaring laughter that found them on their backs, tears streaming down their face. "Help! Help! Come down here and help me at once!" he threatened. Ironically, the animals had suddenly developed selective deafness. They rolled and squirmed in fits of laughter on the ground near the hole. Kasper was growing increasingly frightened in the dark and in his 'stuck' state and anger he yelled "Now!" so loudly, that the floor shook. The obedient animals scurried down the hole as quickly as they could, in one long line. Obliviously, they moved at such speed down the hole, that they banged straight into the furry obstacle head first. Kasper's extensive rear acted as a trampoline and the bemused animals were catapulted back up the tunnel landing on their heads at the entrance of the tunnel.

Panicked, the animals looked around the floor area for something to assist them in unblocking Kasper. Propped against the house was one of the wooden logs to be burnt on the open fire in winter time. The animals struggled to pick up the log between them but persevered angling the log down the hole towards Kasper's ample behind. Off balance the animals tried to pick up speed as they travelled down the tunnel, falling and stumbling under the weight of the log. Picking up momentum as the tunnel descended to the cellar, the animals unfortunately were blinded by the darkness and collided with Kasper's rear with such an impact that he flew out of the exit of the tunnel landing on his head and slid across the dusty cellar floor. A bump on the top of his head began to rise and throb instantly and he felt dizzy as his head spun with the force of the bang.

When he finally stopped spinning, he started to smile as the realisation struck him that he was finally in the cellar and his dreams were about to come true. He positioned himself slowly by the secret hatch as the animals looked on. Kasper could remember every second of the ritual to unlock the wondrous jigsaw piece from its protected place below. Carefully he followed the process patiently raising his paws, saying the strange words and to his pure amazement the jigsaw piece suspended itself before his eyes.

The smile on Kasper's face stretched wider and wider until he was beaming. He picked up the jigsaw piece and placed it preciously into his large furry pouch, made from the abundance of furry skin on his chest. He placed his front paws on his chest and stared wickedly up to the ceiling and whispered wryly...."Now let it all begin."

Forcefully, he pounced past the stunned animals without a glance or word up the tunnel, snatching his hidden bag of belongings and ran off into the distance.

A new ... the rear ... Oh dearly dear..."

CHAPTER 8

Kasper never once looked back. He had dreams, wishes and plans to make a significant difference to so many. Unfortunately for all living creatures this was not a difference that would enhance, more destroy and hurt.

After leaving Old Rufus' house Kasper ran and ran until he could run no more (which wasn't far for someone who dodged running at all costs); until he was in the middle of a vast, eerie wood with a turbulent river running through it. Kasper would have normally been quite scared of the strange noises and the unknown world he was surrounded by. However his newly stolen object had given him increased confidence to do anything that he desired. Exhausted he lay under an aging willow tree beside the raging river. His heart was beating rapidly and he was gasping for breath. He had dropped his bag to the floor and laid his head wearily on it to rest, looking up at the blue sky and wispy white clouds above. He slowly removed the jigsaw piece from his hidden pouch and held it respectfully in front of his face, glaring at it with wide eyes, carefully taking in every tiny morsel of the minute treasure into his memory forever.

After he had restored his normal heart rate, Kasper sat up and stared lovingly at the jigsaw piece in his paw. The realisation that Old Rufus had not passed onto him that one piece of vital information – how to make the piece work - hit him like a jolt of lightning! Unperturbed, Kasper knew that anything powerful enough to alter or save the whole universe must be magical and contain such powers that he truly didn't understand. But oh.... how he was ready to learn! He surmised that if he managed to bring the jigsaw piece back to life, as Rufus had demonstrated, then he was very willing to explore the extent of its powers – with pleasure!

He lowered the jigsaw piece onto the grassy floor around him and began the ritual Rufus had shown him. He closed his eyes and moved his arms cautiously up and down and whispered the strange words... "Deo...Deo...". As he opened one beady eye, expecting to see the piece suspended in the air, sadly he opened the other eye to check that his disappointment was real. Nothing, it just lay there, like a dead piece of coloured worthless wood. He repeated the ritual once more, but louder....still nothing.

Kasper had spent his whole furry life being patient, waiting, waiting, waiting! But right now his patience was reducing by the minute! "Why won't it work?" he thought angrily. "Something so magical should just obey its owner... and that is now me! Kasper K. Itty." His frustrated behaviour was rather amusing to watch. Many of the woodland creatures peeped out from behind their hiding place to see what all the commotion was about. And what a commotion! Kasper continued to try everything he knew to make the piece work. He sang to it, threw it in the air, poked it with his paw, squeezed it, covered it in grass, said a range of 'magical' words that he had read in books and finally jumped on it with four furry paws. Nothing!

Kasper sat down in a huff! He folded his arms, crossed his legs and his bottom lip dropped to the floor. He looked very funny! The animals in the wood had never seen such a hilarious display before. Kasper sat and stared and continued to stare at the piece. He had to work out the next part of his plan — what was he going to do now?

Back home Rufus had returned from his shopping trip. He had made himself his usual cup of tea with one and a half sugars and fell fast asleep in his chair for an afternoon nap. He had absolutely no idea of the theft under his house.

CHAPTER 9

Kasper lay down on his back rather tired and very fed up! He wondered whether he should return home and try to find out from Old Rufus how the piece worked. As he thought, tiredness took over and he fell into a deep sleep whilst thinking and night fell all around him.

Something amazing happened as he slept. We'll let you into the secret that Kasper was so desperate to find. Everything living within the universe is dependent on water. Water is the single most important substance of all which allows growth, health and sustains life. As this jigsaw piece controls the universe and specifically planet earth, water must be the key to the magic within. One drop of water will unlock the power enabling the owner of the jigsaw puzzle one wish and that wish will be granted.

So as Kasper slept that night, the grey clouds of a wintery storm appeared about his head. As morning broke, the first drops of the storm began to fall. Kasper was shaded under the branches of the tree like a huge umbrella.   However one tiny droplet of water fell innocently through the branches landing onto the jigsaw piece, beside the sleeping fur ball.

Immediately as if someone had turned on a switch, the jigsaw piece came to life. It rose from the floor ever so slowly and had a faint blue glow all around it, as it hovered. If you looked closely at the magical piece you could see that the green sections looked luscious and healthy and the blue looked warm and inviting like the deepest oceans. It hovered obediently next to its master, waiting to grant the one wish it was obliged to do.

Kasper was dreaming. He sat solemnly on a golden throne high above the millions of people awaiting his next command. As he drifted back into consciousness he smiled purring as the people below, followed his every breath.

Sleepily, Kasper rolled over onto his back and stretched his furry paws towards the sky one at a time, extending and relaxing his sharply honed claws. His eyes remained closed. The creatures of the woodland that were mischievous as well as nosy, were so intrigued by this strange creature's earlier behaviour, that they had rounded up most of the neighbouring creatures. After all, it wasn't everyday that funny, furry animals came to visit! As Kasper had fallen to sleep the animals had placed a pile of sticky feathers all around him so as he rolled over, he laid in the feathers forcing him to look like a round hen that had been electrocuted.

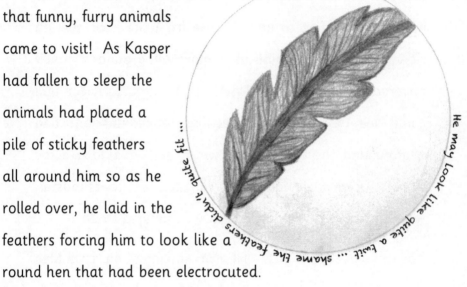

He may look like quite a fool ... shame the feathers didn't quite fit ...

They stood by watching, muffling their giggles.

Eventually, Kasper opened his eyes slowly, welcoming the fresh morning air. As he surveyed his new surroundings he recalled yesterday's events and sighed to himself, knowing he was going to have to return home and face Old Rufus later today.

CHAPTER 10

Kasper could sense something hovering behind his head..... he believed it was another one of those pesky flies buzzing around his whiskers. He waited for just the right moment, jumped heavily to his feet lifting his left paw high to swipe the buzzing nuisance. Just as his paw was about to come into contact with the 'fly,' being sure to send it flying for miles, Kasper's paw stopped just in time, realising that the nuisance was his precious prize. Kasper froze! He stared deeply straight into the depths of the mysterious magical object.

By now, the woodland animals had moved themselves far away from their hiding places. They were hooked on the mystical scene unfolding in front of them. No longer did they find the sticky feathers even slightly amusing. Kasper couldn't speak; he was in a trance. The jigsaw piece had powers so immense that it could crack, kill, explode or heal anything that it desired. Kasper was now under its control. He had ignited its power and majesty. He was the recipient of its awakening.

The magic of the jigsaw piece would enable one wish. To ensure that this was not wasted by lack of thought or a whim, the power looked deep within and granted the deepest desire from the core of the recipient.

Unfortunately for the rest of mankind, Kasper's yearning was to rule the universe; to have some sort of control panel that allowed this ruling to happen. He dreamt, thought and lived for this control twenty four hours each day. The jigsaw piece sensed this and almost instantly his dreams became reality.

The woodland animals continued to look on carefully. As they blinked, the furry hen and the glowing piece of wood disappeared with a flash of blue smoke, never to be seen again.

Immediately, the magic catapulted Kasper high into the blackest sky, millions of miles away from planet Earth. To a place where there were tiny twinkly lights suspended on a black background. In the distance were round balls of varied colours, similar to his dreams, that moved very slowly in a circular motion. Balls of fire shot through the black sky and a huge fire ball roared in the centre of the blackness, keeping the nothingness warm.

Kasper lay asleep on a vast fluffy grey cloud. Behind him was a magnificent, dome castle - similar to an igloo - made from the finest candy floss and an extensive garden complete with a range of mice toys and cat treats, in a rectangular wooden box. The jigsaw piece had also travelled to the cloud but had now lost its glow and was laid dormant next to the sleeping Kasper.

Kasper stirred. As he opened one of his eyes cautiously he saw the blackness above him. His breath stuck in his chest, as he began to panic about where he was just now. He was stiff with fright and his fur (and feathers) stuck on end in fear. Reluctantly, he turned his head to the left and realised that he was laying on something white, fluffy and very comfy. As he rotated his head the other way, he welcomed the view that greeted him, as he saw a beautiful dome castle in its own grounds. Kasper felt a range of emotions. He blinked his eyes hard and poked a sharp claw into his bulging tummy to see if he was still dreaming – after all, this view in front of him was certainly a snapshot of the dreams he had created over the past many years! But strangely enough, he was indeed laid on a cloud, with a castle behind him, somewhere black and lonely. He tried to manoeuvre his ample body from his back to his side but feared that the surface on which he was laying, might not be stable enough. It was after all a cloud and Kasper's only experience of clouds was the white fluffy stuff in the sky that stopped the sun basking his fur.

As he turned he rolled onto the sleeping puzzle piece and pushed it unknowingly through a gap in the cloud. Kasper realised a moment too late that the magical object was escaping his grasp, as he moved his paws towards it. He flipped cumbersomely onto his four paws and stuck his left front paw through the gap, clawing helplessly for the falling piece of wood. But it was useless – it was gone! Floating through the blackness, down....down...down the magical piece fell towards its former home of planet Earth.

Down to Earth it may tumble ... the Earth is sure to rumble ...

CHAPTER 11

It was early morning. Dex and Dood were out seeking adventure. When out together, Dex and Dood looked quite a strange sight! Dex was almost as tall as Dood, even though he travelled on four paws and so to nosy humans it often appeared that Dex was taking Dood for a walk rather than the other way round.

Dex was one of those sniffy sorts of dogs. A beagle to dog boffins or a bugle or master of the sniffs to most. His nose: large, wet and very sensitive hunted food but also adventure and sometimes the odd smelly sock or rubbish bin. He walked with his nose stuck to the floor, sniff...sniff...sniff...sniffing with his bottom and 'happy tail' wagging high in the air, swishing backwards and forwards, signalling the direction towards the adventure.

Sometimes Dex trotted, other times he neither ran nor walked; more of a bunny hop! Or for super speed (used only for adventures), he stretched out his nose and flattened his tail to make himself more streamlined for speed. On these rare occasions, Dood held onto the green rope lead tightly attached to Dex's sturdy neck and was pulled along behind like he was flying! He loved it!

Dexter was only three years old but that made him twenty one human years old – so he was quite a grown up! Whereas Dood was only six in human years and that unfortunately equated to child status! Dex was the brave courageous one of the pair, whereas Dood was a little shy, quiet and sometimes got scared. Dexter always looked out for his buddy and protected him if the need ever arose. Dood however, was the brains behind the duo! So together they made the perfect pack! Dexter and Dood shared one huge similarity! They were both ginger! Dexter was ginger apart from the odd black and white patch, whereas Dood had ginger hair and ginger freckles upon his skin. They both believed that ginger ruled! And this bonded their friendship even deeper.

Today's adventure led them to their favourite place – the enchanted wood. A mass of thick trees, streams, ponds, mud tracks and plenty of hiding places. Dex and Dood had been making a wooden den deep in the wood, near one of the main walkways so that they could spy on passers–by. They had already constructed a rope swing across an extensive valley (soft ground though for swinging accidents) and a walkway between two huge trees, to drop ammunition if ever under attack!

As they ran and flew along the rustic paths they came to Dexter's favourite stopping place: the old, smelly duck pond. He liked to drink the stagnant water whilst checking that the ducks and fish were happy and content this bright sunny morning. Dexter wasn't keen on pure, clean water, instead he preferred water that had a slight green tinge to it (much better for the digestion he felt). Dood sat next to him whilst he drank catching his breath, skimming small flat stones across the water, so that they jumped three or four times across the surface before sinking.

Take a flat stone, watch it bounce ... it's rather funny to watch the frogs pounce ...

CHAPTER 12

Far away in the sky, the jigsaw puzzle piece was picking up speed, as it fell rapidly towards Earth. It had already passed the darkness of the universe, the blazing sun and was now falling through the atmosphere of planet Earth. The small piece of apparent nothingness continued to fall past the clouds, birds, flies, trees and landed on a small lily pad, that covered the surface of a great expanse of water with a little plop!

Fortunately the piece had chosen to land a stone's throw away from Dexter's frantic gulping of water from the pond. Unknowingly, Dex and Dood hadn't realised that something new had landed near them. As Dex continued to drink, he didn't really take much notice of the water in front of him, as he was distracted by Dood's Olympic style skimming technique. The lily pad drew closer towards Dex, as he vacuumed up the water with his snake like tongue until the lily pad finally buffeted into his nose! With a start, he looked up a little shocked and stopped drinking, shook his head, ears and soggy jowls in a propeller head motion, spraying excess water and jowl juice from his mouth all over Dood, the area near Dood and most importantly the sleeping jigsaw piece!

Just as before, the jigsaw piece came to life! It rose gently off the soggy lily pad and switched on its warm blue glow, inviting a spellbound Dex and Dood into its power. They stood there with mouths hanging open. The puzzle piece had one wish to grant to Dexter Dog; his deepest, darkest wish.....to be a superhero!

Surprisingly, Dex began to feel warm all over but he couldn't move. His paws tingled, his ears spun around, his nose stung and his tail felt like it was being pulled tightly and then nothing! As this happened Dex and Dood lay down to relax and fell asleep, seemingly under the spell of the jigsaw piece. Once finished its duties, the jigsaw puzzle had fallen to the ground next to the adventurers. A passing worker ant, collecting stuff for the colony nest, picked up the jigsaw piece, lifted it high above his head rejoined the long trail of workers scavenging in the heart of the decaying matter, on the wood floor.

The wooden piece would make a useful addition to the ant's lair for now.

Sometime later, the adventurers stirred from their slumber and sat up stunned but couldn't recall exactly what had happened to them! Dexter stood up and stretched.

stretching code: bum high ... try to reach the sky ...

His stretching was a bit of an art form; he put his bottom in the air, tail stretched, front paws out in front of him to achieve a full back stretch, then propelling his weight forwards through his shoulders; he stretched his nose, ears and neck as far forwards as they would go (very amusing to any observer)! He felt a bit odd! The adventurers stood up speechless and began to walk home. Dex and Dood had that post adventure feeling. They remembered that something had happened...but what?

CHAPTER 13

Elsewhere, someone evil had settled very contentedly into his comfortable new surroundings. He had moved into the candy floss dome that had every creature comfort possible. A luxury bed with sixteen mattresses, entry to this extravagance was via a tree ladder that he enjoyed climbing. The very best cream, meat, cat treats and numerous kitten servants to jump to his beck and call. He spent his days in his tree house snoozing on his hammock or eating. At the top of the castle dome was an open space, like a balcony, that contained a mysterious control station that Old Rufus had told Kasper about. Mini models of the universe, with different coloured balls all rotating around the small fiery ball. There was a plush chair positioned in the corner of the balcony, where Kasper sat and watched the tiny balls as they moved. He was mystified. The only problem was that there was a piece of one of the models missing. One of the prettiest balls, a green and blue one had a section missing. Kasper recognised this as the piece that he had stolen from Old Rufus. Whilst this piece was missing the control station of balls just followed their ingrained circular pathway and could not be operated or changed in anyway. He longed to move the balls in front of him but they would not move.

As he looked out from the control station, he could see down below the real planets. They followed the exact pathway of the control station and he felt a huge frustration that he could not command the controls, to make the balls move in a different way and then consequently alter the way the real planets below behaved.

Kasper had grown more evil and calculating over the subsequent months, alone on the cloud. He had decided that rather than wanting to play with these balls he would quite like to rid the universe of planet Earth due to the stuffy humans trying to control the feline world, keeping them as dumb pets.

Kasper just knew that this could be perfectly possible if he had the missing piece as Old Rufus had explained, but where was it? He had tried everything he knew to make the balls move but they remained stubbornly routined along their same boring pathway. In pure frustration, he had even taken a running karate jump at them but unfortunately hurt his furry paws, rather than the balls.

As usual, Kasper spent his days lazing away thinking about how he could conquer the universe. Thoughtfully he often planned possible ways in which he could beat the ball riddle and make them move differently. He had searched the whole cloud for the jigsaw piece but it had disappeared. He longed to be the master, the controller of everything, to turn the fireball off when he wanted to sleep, play ten pin bowling with the other balls and be on the front of every newspaper, on every news programme and ensure that every living creature in the universe, did exactly as he said.

One miserable, gloomy evening Kasper was mooching about in his tree house making huffing and puffing fed up sounds; the television was playing repeats of kitten combat, a saucer of cold milk in his paw and he lay swinging in his hammock back and forth. As he snoozed, he dreamt his usual dream of world domination but was rather fretful in his sleep and fell out of his hammock, onto the wooden floor. Kasper had almost doubled in size since leaving planet Earth and so as he fell the whole cloud shook (forcing water droplets to fall from the cloud) feeling the force of his ample size. As he groaned and rolled over, he happened to look under the frame of the hammock. There was something under there that he had never seen before. He cautiously stretched out his paw and retrieved the object and held it out in front of him.

It was an old scrappy piece of paper and on it was an untidy message...

"try the blue windmills on sticks at the bottom of the garden.....STUPID!!"

Kasper read it, a little offended! A wry smile appeared across his face, it was a sign - not an insult. Someone, somewhere was helping him! Maybe he had a guardian angel (lion!) after all, as he had never seen this piece of paper before. Off he pounced, down the stairs, to the bottom of the luscious garden that grew guns, bubblegum, windmills and whoopi cushions.

Carefully he picked one of the blue windmills that was growing on a green stick, being careful not to damage the stick or the sails of the windmill. He couldn't quite imagine how this was going to help him gain control but he was willing to try anything...off he skipped one happy kitty, to the control station.

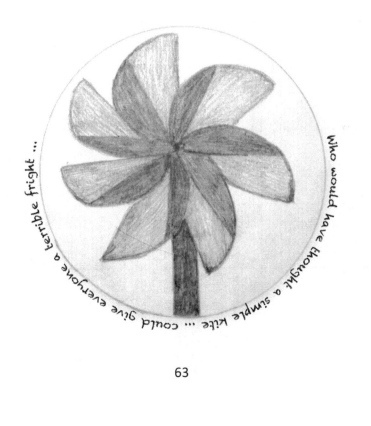

CHAPTER 14

Dex and Dood woke up the following morning feeling slightly stunned. They weren't really sure what had happened to them yesterday but soon forgot as they convened around their adventure planning table, under Dood's bed. Dood and Dex had been devising a plan to retrieve their prized catapult, which during an earlier catastrophe, had become stuck in the crevice between two large rocks high on Highcliff, the highest point in the woods near Dood's house. They were practising their aiming techniques at a couple of smelly girls, when they were rumbled by some crumblies, dropped the offending article and scarpered.

The problem with this retrieval was that they would have to battle extreme heights, weather and a possible fall down the crevice to collect the catapult. But Dex being the brave puppy that he was assured Dood that they would manage the challenge easily.

"Do you think we need a harness or soft landing mattress Dex? You know I'm not good with heights!" Dood shared nervously.

"Nah! I've got four paw drive! We'll easily run up there and collect it. I'll stretch down and grab it with my gnashers. You can keep hold of my tail! We'll be just fine...Don't worry," Dex reassured.

Dood was still thinking the plan through, as they collected some provisions from the kitchen. "Bye Mum, I'm just taking Dexter around the block," he shouted, running out of the back door before Mum could question how long this 'block walk' would take.

Running ahead, Dexter pulled Dood along. He was thirsty for adventure. Into the woods they ran, higher and higher they climbed until they approached the winding path that led to Highcliff. Dood stopped to catch his breath by pulling on the reigns (lead) and Dex came to a sudden halt, panting hard. "Can you see it Dex?" he asked.

"...I think so, it's just popping out over there, near the bird's nest!" he explained, pointing with his sniffy nose. Dood was relieved, he thought some other adventurers may have found his treasure and kept it for themselves.

Up they climbed, until they reached the thickest trees and then the bare plateau at the summit of the rock face. Just like a monkey, Dood held onto the furthest tree trunk with both hands, eyes closed, looking petrified, as he nudged himself closer towards the edge. Dexter had bounced forwards full steam ahead, only putting on the breaks when his nose pointed downwards, into the nothingness over the cliff edge.

"Dexter! STOP! STOP! You're right on the edge, be careful," he yelled as Dexter pounced past him with speed. It was too late, Dexter had not anticipated that the land was about to run out quite so quickly and he had been majorly distracted by Dood clinging to a tree, in quite such a bonkers manner. Dood was so scared but he edged himself closer to the danger zone, determined to help his friend. However Dexter was beginning to fall. It was as if the scene in front of him was happening in slow motion. Dood made a desperate grab for Dex's pointy ginger tail, just missing the white tip on the end by millimetres. Head first, Dexter fell over the edge of the cliff. He tried with all his might to circle his arms and legs like a bird but without feathers and only fur, it was useless. Dood looked on helpless..."Help! Someone help me!" he shouted, panicking. But they were so far away in the woods that no one heard them. Dood's eyes filled with tears as he fell to the ground, not able to look down and see his best friend splattered on the rocks below. Dood sobbed, big deep sobs from deep within.

Curiously as he sobbed, he sensed someone staring at him. He opened one of his wet eyes and closed it tight shut again. He opened the other one slowly, seeing the same sight and shut this eye in the same shut tight way. Dood lifted up his head and opened both eyes.

"Hey Dood why are you so sad?" said a familiar voice in front of him. It was DEXTER! He was there in front of him, with the catapult in the mouth. But he wasn't stood on the ground! He was well....flying! His nose had turned from black, to a sort of flashing light, his tail was rotating round and round like a propeller and most importantly, his feet had some sort of rocket attached to each of them. And there he was hovering in front of Dood! Dood, thankfully, took the catapult and placed it back in its rightful place in his back pocket.

"Coming for a ride, buddy?" Dex asked, beaming from ear to ear; he knew that his wish to have magical powers had somehow come true. Dood's mouth hung open!

"Yer mmmmm I think so!" he stuttered in shock. Dexter guided him carefully onto his back.

"Steer with my ears buddy and hold on tight!" he commanded, seemingly enjoying every moment of this flying experience. Dood was speechless but trusted his friend and did as he asked. Off they rode, down the valley a little wobbly at first. Dood ended up holding on upside down around Dexter's tummy, at one point, when a bit of erratic steering turned nasty. But they managed and they were quite enjoying their first flying experience....that was of course, until they tried to land. Trying to land was a bit like riding a bike: get it wrong and it hurts...LOTS!

"I am getting a bit tired Dood, I think we should try and get back on hard ground!" Dexter explained. Dood was finally having so much fun, one hand on each of the handle bars (ears), making an aeroplane noise at the top of his voice that he didn't hear Dexter's request. "Dood... NOW!" he shouted, bringing Dood's attention back onto the immediate problem of landing. Searchingly, they both looked for somewhere soft to land; rather unfortunately there was no runway available to them.

"There Dex, look...there is a massive field with round balls that look quite soft!" he suggested, pointing to a rectangular yellow field that had been recently harvested, leaving bales of hay ready for collection by the farmer, scattered across the field.

Dood steered Dex like a dodgem car aiming for the field. As a novice flyer, Dex wasn't entirely sure how to make himself go faster or slower, so just like cartoons on the television, he stuck out his back paws to try to create some form of air resistance, to slow them down. This in turn started to tip them off balance and Dood began to panic once more, letting go of the handle bars and placing both arms and legs around Dexter's tummy in a bear hug, closing his eyes and fearing the worst! Dexter came into land very quickly, tail in the air and struck the soft straw head first, pushing him up into the air into a series of clumsy tumbles through the hay bales; leaving Dood and Dex hole shapes cut through the middles before finally coming to rest in the largest bale of all. As usual, Dood was feeling very frightened, sick and scared and now someone had turned off the lights!

"Dex..Dexter...where are you? I'm scared?" he whispered, there was no reply. "DEXTER!" he screamed, in a panic.

"I'm here, squashed flat underneath your hefty rear," Dexter explained through gasps of air, "But what an adventure! Let's go again...NOW! NOW! NOW!" he chuckled excitedly.

"I can't see where we are Dex; it's all dark in here. Can you...?" Dexter had landed completely flat on the grassy surface, with his pointy nose and head resting on the other side of the hay bale. All he could see was bright sunshine and the rolling hills of home. He turned to look behind him, to find his little buddy. Dex could feel him on his back but couldn't see him. Dood was stuck in the centre of the hay bale. No wonder it was dark! He could hear his buddy fretting behind him and put him out of his misery. Full of puppy energy, he stood and embarked on a huge full body shake, from nose to tail. Amusingly, the force lifted Dood from the hay bale over Dex's head and he landed on his back, in the expanse of freshly cut hay in front of him. Dood laid there and caught his breath and slowly filtered the adventure they had just experienced. What did this mean? Were they real superheroes? Would they be challenged by scary people?

As the realisation hit him, he began to feel a little apprehensive. His dreams had just come true! But what would happen next? Dexter on the other hand was doing a celebration dance, circling backwards and forwards chasing his tail and nose, singing a funny little tune about conquering good over bad. Dood sat up bemused and watched his quirky little friend. He was really shocked about what had just happened....but loved every minute!

"Dexter what is that around your neck?" Dood asked, as he noticed a pouch hanging from his sturdy neck. Dexter looked down and couldn't see anything due to his lengthy sniff machine, covering the pouch. "Don't know what you are talking about bud. Did you bang your head?" he jested. Dood got to his feet and walked over to Dexter, lifting the pouch and peering in. Dexter tried to look down in various different ways but couldn't. Inside the pouch was an abundance of pale blue dust that shimmered in the sunlight, nothing more and nothing less.

"There is some questionable blue dust in a pouch around your neck, Dexter...the same colour as your rockets," he explained pointing to Dexter's paws, where the rockets were placed moments before. "Where have they gone Dex?....and your nose has returned to its shiny black colour! I think the magic must have run out, gone away or maybe we broke it when landed...er crashed!"

Systematically, Dexter checked the parts of the body that he could see and with increasing disappointment realised that the magical powers had indeed left him – he was just a dog once more! Even the pouch had disappeared, which they were talking about only seconds before. Determined, he trotted over to one side of the field; put his nose to the floor, pinned back his ears, pulled himself backwards as if he were an Olympic athlete about to respond to the starting gun in the 100m sprint, took a deep breath and off he charged! And he ran and he ran some more! His ears span around as did his tail, but on the floor he remained. He panted back towards Dood and slumped into a disappointed heap.

"It's gone Dood! We had it for two minutes and now it's disappeared!" he explained with desperation.

"Maybe not Dexter!" Dood thought, "As with all superheroes, they turn their powers on and off, so that the crumblies don't realise who they really are. All we need to do, is work out how to turn on your powers. And in the meantime we can plan our superhero outfits! I'm thinking blue Dex, to match your rockets! What do you think?" he suggested, as he stood up to walk in the direction of home.

Sulkily, Dexter stood up and began to follow Dood. He was so disappointed. He wanted to be a full-time superhero. Dex had imagined his name in lights, his picture on every dog bowl in the world, jails full of bad people, fan clubs and concerts in this name. But he would have to be patient for a bit longer and let Dood dress him up in a cloak and mask and then he would start his work. But patience just wasn't one of his strong points and that just made him even more restless.

Dexter dog strong, brave and neat ... he'll help anyone – especially for a tasty treat ...

CHAPTER 15

Elsewhere high above the clouds, Kasper stood impatiently by the control station at the top of his mighty castle, with the blue windmill fixed firmly in his paw. He stood there for some time, using all of his brain power (which was limited) to imagine how this stick could make any difference to these balls. The blue and green planet in the middle of the model, still had its ugly hole, where the important treasured piece should be.

Unhelpfully he tried prodding the balls with the stick but it just bent into a curved shape and then sprung back to its original stick like shape, once the pressure was released. What annoyed Kasper the most was: how the balls continued moving on the same pathway, ever so slowly, day in, day out. But they just wouldn't move for him...not even one stinky millimetre!

After hours of poking, prodding, turning and whipping Kasper threw himself onto the floor in a paddy. Front furry paws and rear furry paws hitting the floor, whilst the windmill flew sharply into the air. He eventually tired himself out with anger and rage. He then turned onto his furry back, gasping for breath and looked up under the control station, with the balls suspended above him. He analysed the balls closely, as he had done so many times previously. Just before he turned to get back onto his feet, something caught his eye, something he had never seen before. At the very bottom of the green and blue ball, was a tiny hole. He leapt to his feet to look more closely. A hole indeed there was! He looked at the rest of the ball and saw the same hole at the very top, parallel with the first. The minute hole ran straight through the centre of the ball and was the exact width of the wooden stick that the windmill was attached to.

With all four paws, he leapt onto the windmill that was now discarded post paddy at the other side of the room. He picked it up and meticulously pushed the wooden stick in the hole, until it poked all the way through, leaving the windmill poking out at the top of the ball. Kasper had noticed a hard icy coating around the hole at the top and bottom but as he poked the stick through, the icy membrane was pierced. All of a sudden, it all seemed clear... he knew exactly what he needed to do. He bounded along to his playground at the other side of the igloo castle and dragged his circular fan to the control station (the fan was normally used for drying his washing). As he plugged it in, the blades began to rotate, pushing cold air onto the blue windmill. Consequently the sails of the windmill began to move in the opposite way to the rotation of the blue and green planet; this caused the stick that ran snugly down the centre of the ball to pull strongly in the opposite direction. As the fan picked up speed, the blue and green ball began to struggle, seemingly fighting against the forces that pushed it to move in its usual rotation. Over the next few minutes, the ball started to move slightly slower, as it fought against the wind and after thirty minutes it had stopped rotating altogether. With glee and delight, Kasper couldn't believe his luck! He hurried over to the side of the cloud to observe what the immense planets below were doing, would they move in the same way or would they be affected by the control station? Kasper watched with excitement, but after a few minutes the excitement faded. The planets continued to move in the slow repetitive way that they always did, not a jot of difference! Kasper looked on and disappointment started to rise within.

He had hoped, believed and dreamed that this control station dominated the whole universe below. But here he stood with the control station well and truly moving in a different manner but the planets below were not responding.

He sank to his furry knees in disappointment, not sure what to do next. He continued to watch hoping and willing for the smallest change.

But nothing....nothing....nothing.... and then it happened! Slowly, very slowly indeed the green and blue planet began to slow down. Hardly noticeable at first, but the rotating was definitely slowing down. Kasper started to smile, the most evil smile; his plan for world domination was about to begin.

CHAPTER 16

Meanwhile back home, Dexter and Dood had been extremely busy. The duo had rushed home! Dood had work to do! He had to dress them and promote them into the greatest superheroes the world had ever seen. Dood had sprinted into his bedroom and scavenged around under his cluttered bed, until he found two already made and well-worn blue cloaks, blue masks, blue t-shirt, combat blue trousers with extra pockets and finally his adventure belt of tricks. Patiently, Dexter waited whilst Dood decided what clothes he should wear – however Dexter believed these superhero clothes made him look rather stupid! He was a loyal companion to Dood and supported his blue theme with a golden D to identify them on their cloaks, but in all honesty he preferred to just dress as a humble dog! Obediently he stood perfectly still, whilst Dood dressed him up in a cloak that frankly made him look like a girl, something he spent his life trying to avoid! This dressing up thing, up to now, had been exclusively observed only by the four walls of Dood's room and the toys who sat lifeless on his shelves. But Dex knew very soon that they would need to introduce the world to Dood and Dexter – awesome superheroes! The problem was, as Dood wasn't terribly confident, what would the crumblies outside the front door of the house think of him and his dog?

However the acquisition of magical powers had given him all the confidence that he needed. Well maybe a little more than normal.

"Right Dex how does it feel? Do you think you will be able to fly and catch bad folk in this outfit?" he asked enthusiastically.

"Dood, do I really have to wear this? What will the other dogs on my patch think? I'll be a laughing stock? I am sure I could fly much better without it?" he explained pleadingly.

Dood looked Dexter up and down with pride. "Oh, Dex, you just look like a real superhero! We have to keep our identity a secret, otherwise we'll be mobbed by TV and bossy crumblies and that is my idea of a nightmare!"

Dexter nodded his head in agreement. He didn't like being told what to do either and so reluctantly agreed to wear the costume (but secretly planned ways of losing bits).

"Okay, dokey! Off we go Dex! Looking for the bad and helping the good!" he shouted walking towards the door of his bedroom.

"No Dood we can't just walk past the crumblies like this! They'll think we have gone mad!" Dexter explained, continuing with his embarrassment.

"True buddy, very true!" he agreed, turning towards his bedroom window (the only other way out of his bedroom). Dexter regretted making the comment instantly. Dogs don't usually leave houses out of windows - that was left to birds or cats without brains! Outside of Dood's window was the vegetable patch, compost bin and Dad's award winning shiny green greenhouse, none of which Dex particularly wanted to land on to. Dood opened up the window excitedly and cautiously looked out.

"Well we aren't going to worry about what is down there Dex because we are going to fly over it!" he explained nervously. "Are you ready to fly again?"

"Yes I am ready Dood or as ready as I ever will be!" he agreed, putting both front paws on the window sill. Dood straddled Dexter's back and checked the contents of his adventure belt before embarking on their adventure. It included water pistol, extendable grabber (used for picking up litter, but much more use as a grabbing implement) potato gun, chewing gum, stink bombs and many other treasures, too many to list.

"Let's go Dex, let's go and find our first crumbly criminal to capture and take to the police station."

Dexter stood there ready. He stood and stood some more. And well, nothing happened. "Come on Dex, whenever you are ready?" Dood retorted impatiently. Dexter had spent the last four minutes trying to think of ways to make himself fly. "Dood...Dood...I don't know how to fly!" he eventually admitted.

Stunned, Dude replied, "What do you mean you don't know! You were flying only a few hours ago! Don't you remember?"

"Of course I remember. But my powers have stopped and I don't know how to turn them back on!" he shared.

Dood climbed off his back, frustrated. "We are so close to our dream Dex. Can you remember what happened when you fell off the cliff? What started the powers working?"

Thoroughly, Dexter thought about each step of what happened but he couldn't recall anything significant. It just sort of started, as he fell through the air.

"Well I think we should jump out of the window, just like you did on the cliff top and as you fall the powers will start," Dood suggested. Strangely enough, Dexter didn't really warm to this idea. What would happen if the powers didn't start? Landing on the pointy greenhouse would certainly give him more than a few bruises. "Come on let's try!" Dood persuaded, with increased confidence, straddling Dexter's back again. "You won't fall, the powers will work, I'm sure! I'll be with you buddy, all the way."

Dexter knew there was no point arguing, this was Dood's dream and Dexter half believed Dood, knowing that this was how the powers had originally started.

They stood nervously on the windowsill, checking that the nosy neighbours had their beaks behind the blinds. They gulped hard, took a deep breath and closed their eyes, pushing themselves forwards so that they tipped off balance, heading towards the floor. Desperately, Dexter tried to circle his tail and ears to start the hovering process. But as they opened their eyes, the view that greeted them was not quite as expected.

The powers hadn't worked! Dex and Dood continued falling to the ground, landing face first into the stinky compost heap. Luckily the pile of decomposing vegetables had broken their fall but they were now covered in smelly bits of food. To make matters worse next door's cat Oscar (the snob) had witnessed the whole episode from the comfort of his velvet basket and was now rolling in his basket, cackling with laughter!

They stood up speechless and walked to the back door. As usual, Mum was rushing through the door late for work — applying her pinkness always delayed her. "Hi darlings," she gushed, "I'm late as ever," she yelled as she ran past oblivious to their dress and dishevelled state. "Remember to wash behind your ears and don't be late for tea tonight, Granny is coming," she continued as she rushed past.

As she ran; she suddenly stopped. Dex and Dood and even the posh cat from next door had felt it. But what had they felt? It was a strange sensation, like the street had started moving in a different way. It felt as if they were being moved in some way from under their feet and that they might fall over.

Dex and Dood ignored the feeling and ran as best they could, upstairs into their room and slammed the door. Instantly they turned on the television to find out what was happening. On every channel was the same image.

A fat, furry ginger cat (Kasper) lay stretched out on a red chez lounge, calmly explaining that what they were feeling was the beginning of a plan to rid planet Earth of people. He was also threatening that things were going to get very tricky for humans rather shortly. The image was on the screen for about thirty seconds and disappeared abruptly, without any further explanation.

Momentarily, Dexter had been distracted from universal domination by a hairy sausage from last night's tea. He was feeling a little peckish and couldn't believe his luck when he sniffed out the smelly hidden prize. As usual, he rolled on the sausage; first neck then down his back, one side of the body and then the other until he was covered in mouldy sausage scent - should he need to hunt down a sausage anytime soon! Finally he woofed at the sausage twice, before munching it down swiftly in one bite!

Dood was very used to this behaviour! As it was a usual Dexter mannerism! But maybe not the required behaviour for a superhero! Dood noted this for an area to develop at a later date!

"Dex this is our moment, our chance to find that big furry cat and show him who is boss! Come on, we need to get going! We have millions of people to save!" he squeaked, as he paced up and down excitedly in his vegetable cuttings, dropping bits on the bedroom floor.

"I quite agree Dood but we have the continuing problem of a lack of magical powers and now the additional problem of not knowing where to find this cat! Give me a scent Dood and I can follow him anywhere," Dexter retorted.

CHAPTER 17

Deep, deep in the woods the worker ants had buried the magical jigsaw piece in their mossy nest, in the heart of a spindly monkey puzzle tree. Unbeknown to the busy ants, that this section of their nest would be instrumental in deciding on whether humanity would continue, whether day would follow night or whether there would be a universe as they knew it at all. Someone had to find this jigsaw piece, both Kasper and Dexter knew of its powers and it would be a race against time to see who found it first.

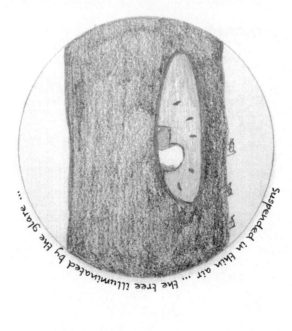

"... the tree illuminated by the glare ... thin air ... Suspended in"

CHAPTER 18

Spritely, the duo of pretend superheroes tidied themselves up, removing the decaying vegetables and decided the best course of action would be to return back to the cliff face where Dexter fell off, to retrieve his powers. They had also agreed not to go out in full superhero costumes, as Dexter had refused to move until he looked different and so they had placed coats over their costumes.

They began their short journey up to Highcliff, along the windy tracks. It was a bit awkward, as they kept falling or tripping due to the strange force acting upon the world, but they were determined to continue.

As they neared the top, Dexter was, as Dexter's do, sniffing the ground checking the smells of all the creatures that had passed these areas over night. He marked his scent as all dogs do! This was his territory and he liked the whole forest to know it! He came across a particularly smelly purple flower, that needed an extra sniff and to his surprise a grumpy bumble bee popped his head out of the flower. Startled, Dexter sneezed. One of those ear flapping, flower flattening sneezes. As he did so, Dood turned round to see Dexter sneeze and the mystery of unlocking the magical powers commenced. A sneeze! Of course! Dexter's nose was his most important feature! Why hadn't he thought of this before? His nose immediately lit up with a glow, the rockets appeared, pouch returned once more around his neck and his tail began to rotate!

"A sneeze Dex!! That is all you needed!" he shrieked in delight jumping, falling, and then jumping in delight. As they looked down over the town, they could see people stumbling, crashing into each other and a general panic starting to develop below them.

"Dex! Just an idea...your nose is obviously dead important when it comes to magic...does it feel any different or anything?" he enquired. Dexter sat down as best he could with the blue rockets fired and ready to go. "Well, for one....my nose is definitely extra sensitive. I can literally smell many smells from far away! Another

other odd thing is...well in the corner of my vision I can see some sort of strange wooden object that looks like a jigsaw piece!" he explained.

"How odd Dexter! I wonder what that means?" Dood asked puzzled, "Maybe it could be a sign! Something that we need to follow or something!"

"I have absolutely no idea Dood, it's maybe just something in my eye!" he replied and changed the subject. "But I could always take off this stupid mask and I'm sure it will go away?" Dood pretended to ignore such a silly statement and Dexter knew he wouldn't win another clothing discussion, now that the powers were working again.

"Right let's go and check out what is happening! It's time to start making a difference! Take off your coat Dex! It's time for the world to be introduced to the universe's more amazing superheroes! Dood and Dexter!" Dood straddled Dexter (by standing on tiptoes), took hold of the handle bars in his hands and off they went, thankful to be hovering away from the shaky ground below.

As they flew across the town and then further afield, what they saw was the same everywhere they flew. DESTRUCTION! The Earth had started to move differently to normal (as I'm sure you know it usually rotates around 900mph at the equator and much slower at its poles in one direction — geography lesson 1.4) and the affect was heartbreaking.

People were injured through falls and accidents, dormant volcanoes had blown their seals, cars had crashed into each other and people were running around helplessly, crying, looking for help and wanting answers to what was happening around them.

The full terror on planet Earth was immense and frightening and if something didn't change shortly, mankind would begin to die.

As quick as a flash ... Millions of cars began to crash ...

CHAPTER 19

High above the clouds Kasper couldn't wait to see the product of his handiwork. He sat on one of his rocket clouds and directed it to fly closer to the green and blue planet. What he saw pleased him no end. Stopping the rotation of the planet had caused complete chaos to all the people below. His plan was working! Next he needed to increase the force to the windmill to make planet Earth move, as well as stop the rotation, so that it edged towards the other planets, especially the fire ball and this way he could begin to rid the planet of horrible humans altogether.

Back he flew to the comfort of home. Another TV announcement first though he thought. A warning! A threat! To let the people below know he meant business. He purred contentedly to himself as he flew. He was indeed, one proud kitty!

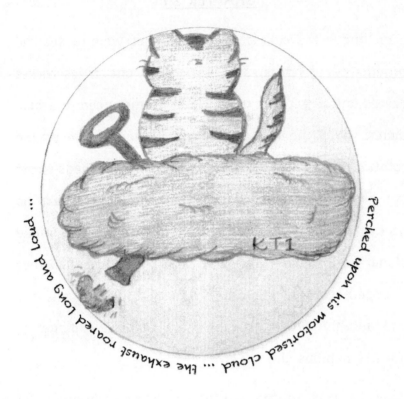

Perched upon his motorised cloud ... the exhaust roared long and loud ...

CHAPTER 20

Like lightning Dexter and Dood had to learn to be real superheroes right now! They couldn't afford to waste anymore time. They had such an important job to do – they believed they were the chosen ones! It was a strange sense of responsibility. They had to use Dexter's magical powers for the good of all the living beings on planet Earth. The only problem was; that they really didn't know the extent of the powers or if these powers would run out at any time.

Dood sat proudly on Dexter's back; holding onto his ears, steering the way. Dexter's nose flashed as he flew, as a kind of satellite navigation, the four rockets blasted and his tail rotated like a propeller. Both Dood and Dexter sported their superhero costumes, disguising their identity, much to Dexter's disgust. The mask kept on slipping down over Dexter's eyes as they flew. He had spent many months using the mask as a catapult, stretching the elastic so that it no longer fit quite as snugly. The cloak with the sparkly 'D' flapped in the wind, slapping Dinky Dood in the face (he wasn't quite tall enough to see over it) knocking him off balance as they soared high above the houses. Unfortunately, the slippiness of the superhero costumes, his tininess and the flapping cloak, had caused Dood to slip down onto one of Dexter's back legs, where he held on like a monkey. A muffled Dood voice shouted "Help! Look Dex there is a policeman stuck head first in a rubbish bin! Shall we go and help him?" Dood pointed and exclaimed in his best superhero voice (secretly glad at the opportunity to move himself back into the hero flying position).

"Yes here we go! Rescue number one!" Dexter agreed, "Just steer me in the right direction."

Dood was a bit stuck from his current position, but he accessed his extendable grabber from his belt in his left hand, grabbing Dexter's left ear applying his best quad bike driving experience to steer Dexter Dog but it was proving a little tricky (maybe he needed a few steering lessons). They had to drop down from the sky and turn left to land next to the policeman. What a simple task it seemed! BUT NO! Dood pulled on Dexter's ear to steer towards the left but he over steered as he didn't have the best view, causing a bit of a spin but a spin to the left nonetheless. Dood let go of the ear and Dexter rather dizzily, stars before his eyes, managed to pull himself upright and flying straight once again!

"That was close Dood! Whatever you do, do it gently!" Dex warned. "I don't feel too well right now, you might see my puppy dinner again at this rate!"

"I'll try my best," Dood gasped as he managed to shimmy himself back up Dexter's legs and shuffle back into his seated position, in the most unsuperhero-like fashion. "How do you think we can go down towards the land again, give me a clue?"

"Have a look around my ears? Are there any controls or a manual in this pouch thing perhaps, I'm getting desperate!" he suggested. Dood inspected Dexter's furry body as the wind blew past them, half-heartedly. Just as he was about to tell Dex that this was a daft suggestion, he found a round dial under his fur at the back of his head, the same ginger colour as his fur – he almost missed it!

Simply, the dial had 'up, **down**, **start** and **stop**' with brightly coloured Dood finger sized buttons next to each direction, similar to a compass. "Dex I've got it! You've grown a dial that has directions! Well done you!" Dood beamed.

"Excellent, let's go!" Dex yelped. Dood pressed **down** quickly, pointing at the upside down policeman, expecting them to start their decent. Unfortunately nothing seemed to be going quite to plan! As he pressed down, Dexter and Dood shot up, vertically towards the sun, like an arrow out of a bow. "Ahh!" they screamed in unison, Dood holding onto Dexter's ears as they climbed higher towards the sky.

"Do something Dood, quick, try the opposite, try **up**, quick!" he said panting. Dood tried with all his might against the force of acceleration and managed with his little finger to press the up button. They froze in mid air. Their stomachs rose into their throats (like one of those cliff-hanger rollercoaster rides) with the stopping motion. Instantly, they turned in mid air and were immediately plummeting to earth at exactly the same speed. "Yikes! This is scary stuff Dood, what are we going to do?" Dex asked, thankful that the mask was now covering his eyes. But they had insufficient time to do anything, as they found themselves heading for the bright yellow bouncy castle belonging to the village show. As they bounced onto the castle with such force, they knocked ten snotty six year olds in their best party frocks onto the grass surround and landed with a bump next door to the screaming policeman - not quite the entrance that they had planned!   Nevertheless, they brushed themselves down, rearranged mask and cloak, placed hands on hips and nose high in the air, united in bravery, ready to tackle the problem.

The heroes caught their breath and ran over to the upside down policeman. Dood stood on Dexter's back to make himself taller, retrieved his extendable grabbers once more from his adventure belt, placed them around the policeman's flapping leg and Dex pulled backwards.

Together they pulled the policeman from the bin and placed him helmet first, onto the ground. Many times, the heroes had planned tricks such as this in the privacy of their bedroom and were very flattered when the two old people, trying to keep their balance and the youth kicking his ball into the strange atmosphere, stopped their battle against their everyday activities to clap at the spectacle in front of them.

Dex and Dood had done it, their first rescue and they loved every magical minute. The ground was still moving strangely around them and the continued destruction was getting worse. Trees were falling, buildings were beginning to crumble and fires were burning down the beautiful countryside. People were running around the streets frightened, looking for solutions to stop the misery. Dexter watched as a startled driver crashed accidentally into another; just metres away from a crowd of bewildered children. Inside the car, the man was stuck and could not move, shouting for help.

"Come on Dood, we need to help that bloke — he is stuck in his car, it might blow up any minute," Dexter retorted, quickly moving towards the disjointed car.

"Too right, D and D superheroes toooooo the rescue!" Dood sang, getting carried away with himself, he swayed and flapped his arms and then sped off in a funny little dance, after his furry companion.

The poor man was well and truly stuck in the driver's seat and all the door locks had jammed with the impact. Dex ran up to the driver's window, put his front paws on the bottom of the window frame giving the man inside a bit of a shock (it isn't everyday that you see a dog dressed in clothes jumping up to your window). Patiently, Dexter tried to tell him to be calm and they would get him out in just a moment, but all the man could hear was angry barks, increasing his anxiety.

Dood reached towards his adventure belt and retrieved his emergency sucker, from its safety holding clasp. He placed it like a javelin over his shoulder and threw it at the window, so that the sucker adhered obediently to the glass. Dexter held onto Dood around his waist, a bit like pulling out the enormous turnip, and they pulled with all their might. Dexter added his tail propeller for extra propulsion and the window finally gave up, with a loud 'POP!'

From his belt he pulls an arrow ... it is long, wooden and rather narrow ...

CHAPTER 21

Kasper K. Itty had been watching from the clouds above with delight, as the destruction unfolded and he liked what he saw. What he didn't like was the interference of two rather stupidly dressed individuals. This had annoyed him greatly and in response, he had decided to intensify the problem below on planet Earth. At the end of his extensive cloud, he had stumbled upon the largest fan he had ever seen, with a label of 'WIND' stuck down its side. With a lot of pushing and pulling and broken planks and weary kitten servants, he had managed to manoeuvre the fan onto the balcony of the control station. He also went back to the garden and pulled the heads (windmills) off four more 'flowers', adding them to the wooden stick that ran through planet Earth, enabling the stick to rotate far quicker, when the high powered fan was turned on. There were three settings on the fan: wind, storm and tornado. He chose to begin with the wind setting only and would increase the power as his plan came together. Once the fan was positioned in the correct place and the wind was blowing in the wrong direction, the result below was that the real planet Earth would begin to rotate in the opposite way to how it has rotated for billions of years – at the moment it was just stood still! (Boring he thought!) He wanted planet Earth to steer off path with more force, directly into the fire ball, but that was his piece de la resistance. Kasper secretly hoped that this may affect the pathway of all of the other planets down below, as they all seemed to stupidly follow planet Earth.

As he turned on the immense 'windy' fan, Kasper began to execute the next part of his plan: getting rid of these two interfering 'heroes'. He jumped onto his rocket cloud and headed for planet Earth.

CHAPTER 22

Elsewhere amidst the chaos, Dood and Dex had just flown across town, to a problem in a dark tunnel that ran a miniature train from one station to another along the countryside, for children usually with their Grannies. The local police and fire service were overrun with problems to fix, they did not know who to arrest or who to save; there were just so many. Everyone was in a flat panic and the problem seemed to be getting worse very rapidly. The police were grateful for their newly acquired helpers, as they could get across towns and cities much quicker than they could. Dood and Dex had wanted adventure but maybe one or two puzzles to solve would have been quite sufficient, not millions and certainly not where people could potentially die.

Up ahead, the tunnel was blocked with rocks as the land had started to crumble and a train full of distraught people was stuck inside the tunnel. Dood had taken his large suction blower from around his waist and had commenced sucking up the boulders away from the tunnel entrance. (Some of the boulders were almost as tall as Dood.) Busily, working as fast as he could to help the stuck citizens, looking behind, Dexter shone the way through the darkness with the light emitting from his nose.

Suddenly as they progressed deeper into the tunnel, the suction noise stopped! As he turned to see what Dood was doing, Dexter realised that he had vanished completely with the suction blower. "Dood come back here! What are you playing at? Have you found someone else in trouble?" he yelled helplessly, beginning to search for him in the nearby area. He looked all around the immediate space but nothing.

"Dex, Deeeexxx....." he could hear from above. As he looked up, he saw Dood's cloak hanging over the edge of a moving cloud; as it rose rapidly into the sky and then it was gone. Suspiciously, three balls fired down from the cloud as an apparent warning to Dexter of water, fire and dust. Dex stood there speechless. His buddy had been taken by a cloud — could this day get anymore weird!?

Quickly Dexter moved the remaining boulders and pulled the train free of the tunnel with his puppy power and four paw drive and flew off high into the sky, to find his buddy.

... fall and fall and ... "Oh no, the bricks will fall ... the pile is increasing ..."

CHAPTER 23

Back at Kasper's pad, high in the sky, Dood had been placed in a cell made from iron bars and a cloud top and base, by an extremely nasty ginger cat (he unfortunately recognised him from the TV and knew he was in massive trouble). Without any explanation or conversation he had been taken from planet Earth, zapped with a strange ball gun so that he couldn't feel his body, floated to a strange cloud and then forced into a cell. "What will Mum say when I don't come home for my tea?" he thought. Without Dexter or his Mum, he sat on the cloudy grey floor and cried. He wasn't a superhero anymore; he was a lonely little boy who needed looking after. He had no idea why this was happening to him or how he was going to get out. He was also worried about the people far below.

Here he is stuck in his cell ... will he get out? Only time will tell ...

CHAPTER 24

Panicking slightly, Dexter flew into the sky circling around planet Earth. He asked the passing birds if they had seen anything of his mini friend. But they all tweeted a conclusive "No." He was growing weary and frustrated. Below him, more and more problems were occurring, but without his buddy he didn't know what to do. He landed heavily in a heap on the top of a mountain, somewhere snowy and cold. The world felt so strange, that he had to place all four paws firmly and grip the solid Earth to stop himself falling over. As he thought through possible ideas of where to look next, he fell quickly into a deep sleep, with his paws holding him securely in position. He had after all, worked very hard today and being a superhero was hard work for a puppy that was used to sleeping ten hours each day.

As he slept he dreamt. It wasn't the usual dream of fighting the bad and conquering evil; today the dream was about a wood, far, far away. In his dream he was watching ants, families of hard working ants, carrying shreds of leaves into a spiky tall tree in the heart of the wood. Deep in the centre of the tree, on an ornate shelf was a strange looking jigsaw piece that flashed every now and then, like a light showing the way for the ants. Strangely the ants seemed to bow down in respect before the jigsaw piece, as they passed – a bit like a shrine. The workers continued their work, over and over never tiring.

Dexter stood up, awakening sharply from his dream. He blinked hard and recalled the strange wooden object that appeared in his line of vision, when he received his magical powers. He had forgotten about it, as he had got used to it just being there. As he focussed upon it, it was exactly the same as the jigsaw piece in his dreams. But what did it mean?

"That's it! I remember now how I got my powers. That strange jigsaw piece hit me on the nose. If I can find it, I can use its powers to grant my wishes and stop the destruction far below," he realised, not knowing where all of these ideas were coming from, "But which tree? In which wood? Where shall I start?"

Clumsily, he flew into the sky and embarked on his journey home. The wood nearest home was where they spent all of their time - that was as good a place as any to start the search. As he flew, he waved and share pleasantries with all the local animals as he flew past — they all knew him! In fact: Dexter was the only flying dog they had ever met. Dexter lowered himself down slightly as he came nearer to his familiar territory. The jigsaw piece in his line of vision started to change slightly; it appeared to grow in size. "Was this a sign? Was the piece going to guide me to the real treasure?" Dexter thought. He turned his head to look for his house and as he looked behind, his body continued flying and dropping height in anticipation of landing. What he failed to do was see the tip of the great oak tree as he flew. He realised the arrival of the tree, as he flew into the trunk head first, then body, "Smack," and he slid down the trunk slowly, stars appearing in front of his eyes once more until he landed in a heap on the floor, cloak around his head and mask around his floppy ears.

The world spun quickly past his half shut eyes. The jigsaw piece in his line of vision had doubled in size and was now flashing. "Ouch! That hurt!" he said to himself, but he was pleased that he was getting closer to the piece, if the sign in front of him meant so. He needed to concentrate on his flying game but being a hound he got so easily distracted. As he lay there, across his nose came a trail of ants, one following the other with pieces of green vegetation lifted above their heads. He followed their trail deeper and deeper into the woods, the flashing piece in his vision was giving him a headache, as it became brighter and more intense. His head also throbbed from the collision and it seemed a long time since he was curled up in his bed back home. He was wishing he was there right now, rather than searching for his dinky friend and a misshaped piece of coloured wood. Onwards the ants plodded tirelessly.

"Come on Dex, snap out of this....the world depends on you!" he thought proudly to himself, puffing out his chest.... "What am I thinking....the world depends on little old stinky me! This must be worth a pass out from the next year of baths and at least three and a half truck fulls of my favourite sausages!" That thought gave him all the motivation he needed to continue through his tiredness, forego his extended sleep times and most importantly save the world! (Oh yer...and find his bossy best buddy!).

Stumbling with the forces upon Earth, nose fixed to the ground, bottom in the air, he followed the final ant along the endless trail, through vines and twigs. It seemed like an age but he didn't want to speak to the tiny creatures, in case a great lolloping furry beast may frighten them and stop him finding the magical jigsaw piece.

Finally, the ant family came to the greatest hollow monkey puzzle tree in the depths of the woods. The puzzle piece in Dexter's line of vision flashed one more time and then completely disappeared. Dexter knew with excitement that he had found the piece in this tree, in front of him. The ants routinely followed each other into the centre of the tree, placing their load into the piles and nests within. At the highest point of the hollow tree, suspended in thin air was the key to the universe, the jigsaw piece and stood on top of this was the Ruler of the ant community. He had a crown placed high on his head and staff in his left hand, speaking to his family of workers. The inside of the tree shook and moved as the forces on the earth began to get stronger and tiny creatures below started to look very frightened.

Amused, Dex watched all of this from an oval shaped hole in the bark of the aging tree. He glued his left eye to the hole and knocked respectfully on the bark.

"Hello Sir!" he addressed the Ruler respectfully; "I need your help. The puzzle piece you are standing on is the most important piece of the universe. I know you can't possibly understand and I'm not sure I do too, but I know I need to take this piece into the blackness of the universe above and hope I can stop the destruction you can see happening around you." A decaying leaf fell onto the Ruler's head and his confident, fierce facial expression started to indicate fear as he looked at the changing environment around him.

"This magnificent piece of wood has protected and fed my family for the last few months – it is very important to us. However, I know something of its magic and know it is destined for a much more powerful force....Can I help you maybe....? You look quite lonely!" suggested the ant.

"Aw...! Would you? That would be so kind! My best bud has been taken by a fluffy cloud (don't ask....I know I sound quite mad) and I really need to find him, I think wherever he is could be the origin of all of this destruction. Hop into my pouch, avoid the powder and you will be quite safe – place the puzzle piece in there too," he directed the ant and he diligently co-operated. Dexter's nose flashed, tail spun and they started to rise off the ground. As they turned, they realised that they weren't alone; an old man had appeared through the trees.

CHAPTER 25

Old Rufus Rule had followed the same route through the woods every day. Since Kasper left; he had panicked, sobbed and worried that he had failed in his life-long quest to protect the universe. He hadn't slept, eaten properly or rested, as he was so sincerely worried about what Kasper would do with the jigsaw piece. Rufus could feel the world changing and he firmly believed that Kasper had taken the piece to devise an evil plan, to trigger the demise of the universe. All he could do since that day was search and search and he would not rest until he succeeded.

Dexter felt frightened. Rufus was a towering, powerful man who appeared unkempt and weary. "Er....Hello? Can I help you?" Dexter spluttered. (Rufus for some reason could understand Dexter's words.) Old Rufus took a deep breath and stepped forwards strongly. Dexter cowered towards the tree. However as Rufus spoke; Dexter could sense the warm compassionate man in front of him.

"I am Rufus Rule – Protector of the Precious Piece of Devine Creation...and this has been taken from me," he shared hanging his head in shame, "my whole life has based around being protector of this life sustaining tool and I have failed.....my pesky trusted cat tricked me and stole it." Exasperated Rufus fell to his knees and began to shake as he sobbed. "You can't understand its power....."

"I do!" Dex interrupted as a tree toppled in front of him, "I really do and you can fill us in with the detail. I have the piece you describe and you can help us foil this ginger fur ball once and for all," Dexter pointed to the pouch around his neck and beckoned Rufus to sit on his back, preparing himself for flight.

CHAPTER 26

Far, very far away, upon his wispy cloud, Kasper lay on his maroon chez lounge in front of the rectangular cell that was Dood's new home. Two servant kitties fanned their master and placed the finest sardines into his gaping mouth.

The powerful control tower stood majestically to Dood's right and the wind force that was controlling the movements of the planets, was placed next to it. Dood could see exactly what Kasper's plan involved and he watched horrified, sick with uneasy helplessness. From his imprisonment, he watched the planets below and recognised that Earth was indeed moving differently to all the other planets. His cape was ripped to shreds like seaweed, his belt had been confiscated (apart from his prized catapult which was hidden down his combats) and his hair was increasingly dishevelled through the lost battle to force him into the suffocating cell. He looked like a little lost orphan; the superhero status had long gone!

Kasper hissed, "My plan is almost complete....you will push the final button to make the fire ball and the blue and green planet collide with each other, destroying all the disgusting earthlings on that worthless planet. You....you...the SUPERHERO! Will be responsible for ending mankind...HA...HA....HA!" he smiled the most wicked smile, pleased as punch with himself.

Attentively, Dood listened to the wicked words emitting from the evil creature. Unfortunately he did not fully understand the impact of the control tower and how it was affecting all of the planets, humans and creatures below. He imagined Mum, Dad, Sophie and Olivia would have returned home from work and school early by now and suspected that most of the houses on planet Earth, would have habitants who were either hiding under the kitchen tables clinging onto the spindly legs or hiding in cupboards under stairs.

With venom, Kasper clicked his paws and the bars to the cell disappeared. He pulled Dood roughly from the cell by the scruff of the neck and marched him over to the towering control station.

"Look over there Dood or is it Doodles or something equally ridiculous," he snarled pointing to his servants; "Those kitties and myself have found the most wonderful contraption here on this fluffy cloud, the machine that makes the wind forces we feel on planet Earth. Currently it is on the 'wind' setting and as it exerts its power, it moves Earth on this control tower, corresponding to the real planets below. You are going to turn the settings to 'tornado' where we will see the planet not only rotate in the opposite direction but Earth will be forced to behave in a completely different way, colliding with the fire ball and BOOM! Earth will be gone forever!" Dood stood solemnly watching the real planets below, Earth was fighting the historical forces it had known for billions of years; helplessly things were about to change forever and he could do absolutely nothing about it.

"Fetch me my mirror!" he commanded rudely. Two frightened kittens ran off to collect the oval, golden reflector and placed it directly in front of Kasper. "Yes I'm ready....let's let the whole world know what is about to happen....let the games commence!"

Kasper turned regally to the television camera, puffed out his chest and smiled his widest grin. He had somehow back combed his fur and now looked like he had been electrocuted, "People of the world," he explained, "the time has come for planet Earth to be written into the history books. Take a seat and view the sky, you will see that Earth will very soon become very familiar with the fire ball you use to heat your planet, as you get much closer you will most certainly be fried to a crisp!! Get out your sunglasses, sun cream and fire jackets....You will definitely need them! Watch the planets behave like small, bouncy balls as they change and collide! Oh what fun will be had! Only I Kasper K. Itty have the power! Goodbye Earthlings....Goodbye!" He finished the transmission, sat down on his cloud, so overwhelmingly pleased with himself he could burst!

125

Channels one, two, three and four ... That cat is everywhere – what a bore! ...

126

CHAPTER 27

Poor Old Rufus wasn't too fond of flying. In fact flying made him feel rather sick. Unfortunately Dexter was still only on flying lesson number three and definitely required 'L' plates and a warning light. Rufus had closed his sleepy eyes and held onto Dexter around his tummy, as he had slipped off his back after a near miss with a bridge. The ant Ruler luckily was a rather clever ant and had squeezed himself out of the pouch and placed himself on the control dial on Dexter's neck. He had never driven a dog before but he was a quick learner and rather soon they were flying upwards towards the planets, ensuring that they avoided hitting any more obstacles. Dex was rather glad as his nose was feeling rather sore from all of the collisions. Luckily all of this distracted him from the worrying feeling he had in the pit of his stomach about Dood and what was about to happen.

"We need to find a person on a cloud...Let's go!" Dexter suggested rather unhelpfully, pointing in every direction at the abundance of clouds around them. "That is all I know....."

"NO, I know who that person is," Rufus interrupted. "It is my wretched pet cat Kasper. He stole the magical jigsaw piece that you have in your pouch."

"Now that is funny Mr Rufus but I know that cats are just dumb purr boxes who scratch furniture," Dexter scoffed as his ears flapped in his eyes, "they don't have enough brain matter to steal, apart from maybe fish or mice!"

Old Rufus looked up at Dexter from beneath the rocket paws in disbelief and Dexter momentarily looked down at Rufus, as he was distracted by his glare. Unfortunately this momentarily lapse was enough to make the flying machine nose dive off course once more and down to earth they hurtled! The Ruler ant whose name happened to be Ayvree, tapped Dexter on his head with all his might and managed to regain calm flying once more.

"Can you talk about this when we land Sir?" Ayvree squeaked, "otherwise I fear for my dear life – I have millions of ants to lead and cannot afford to be harmed in any way," he concluded. Dexter and Old Rufus felt like they had been told off by someone really important and stopped talking, focussing on the journey into the night sky.

The adventurers hadn't been travelling long when Rufus shouted, "Please stop! We must stop a moment! I have an idea to help us find the exact whereabouts of Kasper. Silly me, I don't know why we didn't consider it before...I'm so foolish!" he gasped seeming very annoyed with himself. Ayvree looked at Dexter, considered the request and then in apparent agreement turned the dials appropriately (he seemed to have mastered the opposite direction/greater speed problem that Dood had encountered – perhaps due to his regality and importance) to temporarily 'land' them on a tremendously high mountain, topped with fresh snow. Simultaneously the rockets on Dexter's feet fired to a halt and Rufus gathered himself together, regained an upright position, rather red in the face, he sat next to Dexter.

"Let me briefly explain," he panted, "that jigsaw piece that you have all encountered has powers so magnificent that we cannot fully understand. Its power is so phenomenal that it can take life, sustain life and create life and is responsible for everything we know, feel and see. Kasper: the evil monster who has stolen your friend, whilst residing in my home, saw its power as I had the lifelong responsibility to shield it from harm. This was passed down from my Father and Grandfather and until this point, the world has always been free from destruction and threat as it has been protected so fiercely. Sir, Ayvree, if you would be so kind to pass the piece to me, I can ask it to show us the way back to its maker — the control tower of the whole universe."

Quickly Ayvree opened the pouch around Dexter's neck and Rufus pulled out the coloured wood, which was now covered in blue dust from the pouch, as if it were a precious load. As the piece became visible they all realised that it was flashing. It rose obediently from Rufus' hand and placed itself on Dexter's nose. "The flashing will become more frequent and brighter as we get closer to the control tower. I suspect that this is where we will find Kasper and if I was a betting man, I believe the problems on Earth all stem from him stumbling across the control station. Now come on, let's go, you can see below us that we haven't got long before the world crumbles into smithereens," Rufus gently explained in a knowledgeable manner.

The trio only had moments to observe their surroundings below. Trees were now blocking roads, cars had exploded, power cables were snapping and lights no longer worked, projecting countries into patches of darkness and the screams were piercing for all to hear. The picture below was heart-breaking. A tear filled Dexter's eyes behind his blue mask.

Dexter ignited his rockets once more and the jigsaw piece flashed. Rufus and Ayvree took their positions for flight once more. All three were determined to squash this kitty once and for all.

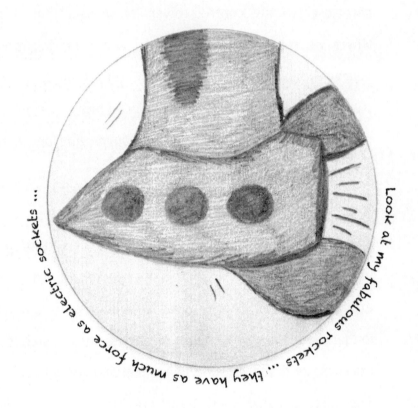

CHAPTER 28

Millions of kilometres above, Kasper had now returned to his superior position on his golden throne that was full of treasures, behind Dood and the 'wind' making machine. Reluctantly, Dood stood next to the machine that was already blowing such a strong force from its sails onto the control tower, watching the reluctant displacement of the differently coloured balls.

"In moments, you will increase the power from this machine by flicking the switch to 'tornado'...the accelerated force generated will push the Earth ball off its usual rotational pattern and will make it collide directly with the fireball and BOOOMMMM! that will be the end of earthlings as we know it!" Kasper spoke now, pacing up and down his cloud, tail whipping viciously with excitement. He rubbed his paws with glee and smiled the widest victorious smile.

Dood couldn't move. He felt numb to the bone. He was going to be forced to destroy the planet where his family and friends lived. It seemed like such a long time ago, that he left his house and an even longer time since he had eaten, but none of that mattered now. He actually found himself missing Mum and her pinkness and would really like a cuddle just now (not a Granny + wart kiss though!)

Moments later Kasper rose from his seated position, looked at the mouse shaped watch on his wrist, and checked the planets below and shouted..." The time has come, pull that switch NOW! Five,four.....three....two....."

"Wait...Wait!" Dood squeaked. "I can't comfortably reach the switch, I'm sure you wouldn't want me to mess up such an important occasion. Could I borrow one of your mouse shaped marbles from your throne, to help me pull the switch, my hands aren't very strong? The hook tail will help me pull it down securely," (Dood had a plan....but would the silly kitty fall for it?)

"Urm...why, why can't you just pull it down stupid boy, try it NOW!" Kasper spluttered, becoming increasingly frustrated. Cleverly, Dood pretended to pull with all his might but could not securely grip his fingers around the

switch as he was so small and
light-weight, the switch
remained unmoved. Kasper
jumped up and down like
a pogo stick in rage and
jumped quickly over to
the throne, collected one
of his favourite marbles and

rolled it across the floor to a waiting Dood. He caught it
quickly in between his fingers.

CHAPTER 29

The flashing on Dexter's nose became so rapid that it was giving him a severe headache. Suddenly in the distance, they could see an enormous grey cloud with, what looked like an igloo in the middle of it. Ayvree squeaked, "That must be the place, look at your nose!" he exclaimed pointing at the bright blue object at the end of an already flashing nose. (Dexter could really appreciate how Rudolf must feel at Christmas time!)

"I think you had best slow down Dexter. We are almost there!" Rufus shouted.

Dexter wasn't listening. He was thinking about last Christmas; his stocking full of sausages and his comfy new bed. He flew full speed ahead. Fortunately the puzzle piece had taken over the control of the flying and consequently everyone had had a much more pleasant experience.

Ayvree stood on top of Dexter's head with the poise of a sergeant major. "Right I have a plan and it goes like this....Dexter I want you to move forwards and hover under the centre of the cloud, so that we cannot be seen. We need to look for a hole in the cloud near this control thingy for me to sneak through! Can you do that?"

"Yep I think so, or I will be able to with the help from this amazing object on my nose. I have never been so impressed with something so small in all my life!" Dexter explained.

Above the cloud, the marble had been received gratefully from the foolish Kitty. Fortunately for Dood, he had remembered his prized catapult that he had hidden down his combats and he was a pretty good shot with a catapult (not Olympic standard; but the best on his block). As he received the marble, he placed it dutifully in his hand and slowly hooked the marble around the switch and pulled the switch down from 'wind' to 'tornado'. This act managed to distract Kasper sufficiently to execute his plan. With mixed celebration and immediate concern, Kasper moved alongside the wind making machine, as the increased power input from low intensity to high was far greater than he expected.

The whole cloud began to jerk violently with the force but Kasper remained firm, as his servants ran for cover in the shed at the bottom of the garden. He looked over the side of the cloud, eyes fixed on planet Earth willing it to move just an inch towards the fire ball. The anticipation in his tummy was overwhelming... "Come on Mr Earth move towards your maker..." he hissed.

Spritely, Dood whipped out his catapult from his combats, unhooked the marble from the machine and placed it into the elasticated sling. He pulled it back with all his might and aimed for the back of Kasper's head. Kasper had forgotten about his prisoner whilst he was observing the planets below and had turned his back towards him.

Dood lined up the catapult with increased accuracy, but his hands were shaking with fear and the jerkiness of the cloud was extremely distracting. He took aim and FIRE! The marble hit Kasper full forced on his rear! Ouch! Kasper felt like he had been shot! "Take that you pesky mouse snatcher!" Dood exclaimed, pleased as punch with himself. In extreme pain, Kasper fell into a heap on the cloud, holding onto his rear with both front paws. He looked like he had been scalded!

Meanwhile, all the screaming and shouting had made the alignment of Dexter under the cloud much easier. With efficiency, he hovered under the cloud anxious to see Dood again; he tried to look through the wispy holes in the clouds but they kept moving. Ayvree, as planned, stretched through the cloud carefully.

"Wait a moment? Take some of this with you....cover yourself with the magic dust from the pouch. It will help you along your way, just ask it to help and it will!" Rufus suggested. Ayvree quickly covered his tiny body, with insufficient time to question the information passed from Rufus.

"Be careful up there!" Dexter whispered to Ayvree and he held his nose up high to allow the tiny ant access onto the cloud.

The monstrous fan had started its work. Catastrophically, planet Earth was now moving slowly towards the fire ball. It was slowly spinning in reverse and also moving like a magnet towards the centre of the universe; where a meeting with the fire ball would most certainly end in an almighty explosion.

The sun and Earth will soon collide ... the world as we know it is sure to divide ...

CHAPTER 30

Violently, the cloud continued to jolt back and forth as the powerful fan executed Kasper's evil plan. Kasper, who demonstrated how much of a coward he really was, continued to squirm and yell in pain on the edge of the cloud. He did not notice Ayvree pop his head through the cloud and scurry towards the control tower. The clever ant knew what he had to do but he just hoped he was strong enough to do it; somehow the dust gave him confidence.

Panting, Ayvree scurried along the balcony to the control tower, where he found Dood desperately trying to stop the fan working. But the switch was stuck. It was as if an evil force was protecting the cloud from goodness and that the plan was going to succeed whatever the cost! Sweat was pouring from Dood's face as he tried everything to stop it. Dood didn't notice the tiny ant at first, as he scurried up the metal sides of the control station, leapt onto a ball named Mars, then Mercury and finally onto the green wooden stick running through the green and blue planet.

After fifteen minutes of pitiful squirming on the floor and a realisation that no one was going to come and help him, Kasper stood up. The apparent pain in his rear now subsided. He awkwardly moved towards the edge of the cloud, just in time to watch planet Earth moving rapidly towards the fire ball. Kasper jumped up and down with glee! "Yippee!!" he shouted, "Yippeeee – dooody – deee!" He started to embark on the most ridiculous dance even Dood had ever seen in celebration, which was rather a mistake.

Unfortunately Kasper was oblivious to the events happening around him. He was unaware of the genius ant swiftly moving up the wooden stick towards the windmills, that were making the planet move differently. Dood had noticed what was happening by now, but was a little speechless, so he stood and watched a blue ant executing a rescue plan. Bravely Ayvree jumped systematically onto all of the spinning windmills, one at a time, without any fear. He should have been torn to shreds. However, the magic dust protected him from harm. As he jumped, the windmills disconnected from the stick and spun with speed away from the stick into the air. In unison this repeatedly happened to all of the windmills attached to the stick. As they flew through the air with purpose, they were heading for someone completing the fifth circuit of a strange chicken dance. Five windmills swooped towards Kasper, picking him out of thin air, pushed him with extreme force towards the cell that was Dood's prison and attached him by his paws and tail to the bars of the cell. The windmills acted like chains, pinning him firmly so that he could not move.

"I have no idea who you are...but that was brilliant!" Dood said to Ayvree, pushing his hand forward to shake his in a greeting. Unfortunately Ayvree couldn't quite say 'Hello' in such a way with him being quite so tiny, so he jumped on Dood's hand instead.

"Your clever dog is just below the cloud too, in case you were wondering what is happening!" Ayvree shared, "But we still need to stop these planets moving, Old Rufus needs to come up and sort this I think."

"Rufus? Planets? This really is all new to me, but what an adventure!" Dood exclaimed under his breath.

"Please run over to the centre of the cloud and look through it until you see your dog and an anxious old man... ask them to come here immediately?" Ayvree commanded.

Without hesitation, Dood ran over to the identified point and looked down. There was his buddy, the friend he loved more than any other. He reached through the cloud and patted him fondly on his head.

"Hey Dex! I've missed you buddy! No time to catch up now....that really clever ant asked me to get you Sir, is it Rufus? He needs you?" Dood explained, "Something about planets moving fastly?"

"I'll stay here Rufus!" Dexter offered, "You climb up onto my back and step though the cloud but be careful as it

144

doesn't look very strong...do you want some of this powder?"

"Thank you Dexter, but I will take the piece from your nose and I will be quite safe with this. It will protect me from harm," Old Rufus explained in a calm voice.

The old man clumsily stepped onto Dexter's back and then his head, squashing his ears and his eyes but he tried to keep himself as still as possible. Dexter had no idea what would happen next. Below him, he could see that planet Earth continued to move rather swiftly towards the fire ball and within about thirty seconds it would crash directly into it, unless it was stopped. Frightened, Dexter pulled his mask down over his eyes as he didn't want to watch what could potentially be the end of his life too. All he could do was hover and wait.

Close my eyes and pull down the mask ... especially when the job is a frightful task ...

145

CHAPTER 31

Old Rufus ran as quick as he could to the control station that he was taught about many, many years ago. He stepped carefully up towards the blue and green planet, took out the precious jigsaw piece and took a rather deep breath. Unknowing what might happen next, he slotted the piece into place on planet Earth. Suddenly everything went black!

The jigsaw piece is back in place ... let's fix the problem; no time to waste ...

CHAPTER 32

They all gulped hard! In the darkness, they froze not sure what to do. The floor underneath them appeared to weaken and Dood, Ayvree, Dexter and Old Rufus found themselves falling! Down and down they fell through the darkness. Where were they going?

Cleverly with his long, curly pink tongue, Dexter licked some of the dust from the pouch and wished for a magic flying thing to catch them. He closed his eyes (even though it was dark) and wished the same thing over and over. Cautiously he opened one of his eyes and as he did, as if from nowhere, a carpet flew towards him and hovered under his body until he finally fell onto it. It then darted to the right collecting Ayvree, to the left for Dood and finally swooped a few metres to catch Old Rufus (he was a bit heavier than everyone else!)

As they did, the fireball appeared to ignite once more! "Woooow! How cool was that?!" Dood exclaimed, finding the whole situation unbelievable.

Old Rufus looked carefully over to the planets in the distance. With relief he could see that the contents of the solar system were indeed rotating and moving as they once were. Planet Earth appeared unharmed from where they hovered, however they were unaware of the impact of Kasper's meddling and would have to wait in anticipation, until the carpet lowered further.

Dood and Old Rufus lay on the carpet looking up into the vastness, catching their breath. "What about Kasper?" Ayvree squeaked, "He was left on that cloud that has now disappeared, I hope he is unharmed even though he needs to learn a very harsh lesson!"

Concerned, Dexter looked below the carpet trying to search for him in the vastness so that they could rescue him. But he was nowhere to be seen.

Just as the foursome were about to head back to planet Earth, Dood spotted something in the distance. "What is that?" he quizzed to Dexter.

"I don't know but it is moving rather rapidly towards us?" Dexter answered.

All of the residents on the carpet faced the flying object and squinted to try to see what was coming. As it got closer, they could see exactly what it was. Rather unfortunately it was Kasper on his remaining rocket cloud, racing towards them.

"Ha, Ha!!!" he shrieked to the people on hovering carpet, "I freed myself, I knew you couldn't stop me!" as he passed.

Old Rufus shouted, "It's over Kasper, the planets are back to normal now, your plan has been foiled... Go back to Earth and find a sweet lonely lady to be pampered by; you aren't welcome in my house!"

"You may have stopped me this time, but I will be back and look what I have.....?" he mocked, holding up the jigsaw piece in his filthy paw.

"How did you.....?" Rufus spluttered at the back of Kasper's head, as he sped off into the empty sky. Quickly Dood searched his pockets for his trusty catapult and Ayvree offered to be the bullet. The brave ant covered himself in dust for the final time, as Dood fired the shot of his life gently but firmly as he could. Expertly Ayvree hit Kasper's hand hard enough to release the grasp and the jigsaw piece began to fall through the expanse, heading for planet Earth. Kasper tried to grasp the tiny object but it was useless. He looked back at Dex and Dood as he sped off – they knew that this wasn't over yet! It was too late and too small to even consider catching the jigsaw piece from the carpet. Down and down it fell, where it would lie, nobody knew?

Ayvree too fell to the Earth. Helplessly the people on the carpet could do nothing, as he too was so small and moved swiftly. Suddenly a parachute was pulled from its safety bag in the distance and they saw a faint wave as they knew Ayvree would return safe and sound to Earth in a few hours.

Kasper was defeated and sped away into the distance – but he would be back! They all knew that!

The magic dust strikes again ... a parachute is far more exciting than a plane ...

CHAPTER 33

And there we have the end of our tale! Dexter was left in charge of flying the carpet, as he was such an expert at flying! Unfortunately, he had run out of puppy sustenance by now and was so hungry that he couldn't possibly consider flying anything and consequently fell into a deep sleep. Dinky Dood was also feeling rather exhausted, he hadn't quite realised that being a superhero would be extremely tiring and so he lay on the carpet for forty winks too!

Old Rufus was left. We don't know very much about Rufus and my guess is we never will! A rather mysterious man indeed! With a twinkle of his eye, Rufus landed the carpet safely at his house, once more. The destruction caused on planet Earth had somehow miraculously been reversed – intriguingly Rufus knew that it would be?!

Dex and Dood returned to their front lawn. Eventually, Mum found them soundly asleep under the old oak tree, with their worn and ripped superhero costumes. The world wasn't quite ready, as yet, to be introduced to the newest crime fighting team on the block. So we'll keep it a secret for a little longer.

Instead Mum awoke them and asked, "Are you coming for tea Joseph? It's getting cold?" oblivious as ever.

The heroes stood up, stretched and shook! Wow! What an adventure! As Dexter got up he could feel a sneeze coming on.....

On to the next adventure - no one knows... Who would have thought a sneeze ... could make us feel at ease ... Where will the magic go? ...